R01000 477744

DATE DUE
4 1U 88
3 28 89 8

FINE FOR OVERTIME

DENVER PUBLIC LIBRARY

CHILDREN'S LIBRARY MAIN

js 636 st
Slote
Stranger on the ball club

W9-BVT-393

Stranger
on the
Ball Club

DENVER
PUBLIC LIBRARY

SEP 1971

CITY & COUNTY OF DENVER

Alfred Slote

J. B. Lippincott Company

Philadelphia and New York

G187581

R01000 47744

Copyright © 1970 by Alfred Slote
ALL RIGHTS RESERVED
Printed in the United States of America
LIBRARY OF CONGRESS CATALOG CARD NUMBER 70-117241
First Edition
TYPOGRAPHY BY ELLEN KAGAN

iS 636st

contents

Stranger
on the
Ball Club

»1«

Finders Keepers

Going home I decided to cut across the park. We had only moved to Arborville two days before, but I knew all the good shortcuts already. Sampson Park was my favorite, even though Sampson School was at one end of it.

There weren't many people here at this time of the day; it was a cool April afternoon and getting near suppertime. A few tennis players were punishing themselves on the courts at the far end, and there were still some little kids on the swings and the usual two or three dogs chasing each other in circles.

The park groundskeeper was still there, cutting through the high spring grass with his noisy power mower. He could ignore the ball diamonds, though, because kids kept the grass down by playing on it.

I walked toward the little hill behind which was a path through some backyards that led onto Granger Avenue.

A small white stone sat in the grass in front of me. I kicked it and it skipped over the blades of grass and hit a tree trunk. A good soccer shot. I'd have to learn to play soccer in this city. That's all the fifth and sixth graders did before the first bell rang in the morning and at noon. We'd never played soccer back in Illinois.

Another stone was perched in front of me. I kicked it and it skipped about ten feet and struck something sticking out in the grass. Something brown. I walked over to examine it. Of all things, it was a baseball glove. I picked it up. An expensive, broken-in ball glove. You could still smell the oil on it. A Pete Rose model. It must have cost some boy at least twenty dollars. And he'd left it behind in the grass . . . just like that.

I looked around. The only person nearby was the groundskeeper, and he had his back turned to me.

Finders keepers, I thought.

I tucked the glove under my arm and kept going until I was out of the park, through a backyard, and onto Granger Avenue. Then, on the sidewalk, I examined my new glove more carefully. I turned it over and found a name written in ink on it: "Tad Myers."

Tad Myers?

I tried to put a face to that name. Someone in fifth grade. But I was new here, new to Sampson School and no face I could think of, at least in fifth grade, matched the name. That really made it finder's keepers then. Besides, I was going to need a good glove if I was going to make a Little League team in this neighborhood.

Actually, I'd heard there was no regular Little League organization in this city. The kids' baseball leagues were organized by the city's recreation department, but they ran on the same principles as the Little Leagues. Fathers coached, and you got uniforms, but you were sponsored by different businesses in town and the names of your teams were the names of the businesses. The big difference was that there was no such thing as a farm system. Everyone got a chance to play with the best players. If there were too many kids, they just created more teams.

That suited me fine because back home in Illinois I'd never been able to move up from the farm system. I had a good arm and everyone said that if I learned to hit and field decently and learned to control my temper, I'd be pitching shut-outs for a major Little League team. But before any of that had a chance to happen, my dad decided to move us from Illinois to Michigan.

I didn't want to move, and I don't think my older sister Jane did either. But my father said we had to. He didn't want to live in Peoria anymore, and especially in our old house. It had too many memories of our mother. When a job offer came that meant moving to Michigan, Dad took it. So here I was, trying to make friends with strangers who weren't friendly at all. Yesterday, my first day at school, they had left me out of the soccer game because I didn't know how to play. I was counting on baseball to help me make friends. I was a pitcher—at least Dad said I had a strong arm. He taught me a lot of things about pitching before Mom died, but then he became a lot more quiet and there was less time for us to do things together.

Still, I remembered most of what he had taught me about pitching, and I hoped my hitting would improve. With a glove like this one my fielding had to improve!

So thank you, Mr. Tad Myers. You did me a favor losing your glove in the park. And just to make sure your glove stays lost, the first thing I'm going to do when I get home is get rid of your name.

No one was home when I got there. I leapt up the stairs two at a time and went into Jane's room. She was taking an art class in junior high and had lots of special drawing pens and black ink. Opening her desk, I found a pen and carefully blocked out the name "Tad Myers"—a little black block for "Tad" and a bigger block for "Myers." It was neat. I sat there and admired it for a few minutes before it dawned on me that it wouldn't work. Anyone picking up my glove would want to know what was beneath the two ink blocks. I'd have to do something else. But what?

Then the idea hit me. Since everyone made different hippie designs these days, on their cars, their bicycles, their school books—why not make a lot of odd little blocks on this glove?

Dipping the pen in the ink, I made a bunch of little ink blocks all around the glove and now it no longer looked like just two blocks hiding someone's name.

I was so busy doing this I didn't hear my sister Jane come in.

"And who gave you permission to use my room?" she asked. I should explain that Jane and I fight a lot. We got along better before Mom died, but now Jane has decided she's going to be my mother and boss me around. And she's only thirteen!

"No one gave me permission," I said. "I didn't know I had to have permission to use your room."

She wasn't mad, not yet. But she'd get mad as soon as she saw I was using her pen and ink.

"Put that down immediately!"

"Sure. I'm done anyway."

"What have you been up to, Tim Foster?"

"I'm becoming an artist. How do you like my hippie baseball glove?"

She took it from me. "Where did you get this glove?"

"I found it in the park."

"I don't believe you."

"What do you mean, you don't believe me?"

"Just what I said. I don't believe you and I've got a good idea now what you're doing. You stole this glove and you're covering up the owner's name with my ink."

It was so close to the truth, I was startled. And then I got angry, because I hadn't stolen it, and that was the mean part of her remark.

"I didn't steal that glove."

"You did too. I can see it in your eyes. You're lying. You stole it. You're a thief."

I hit her as hard as I could on the shoulder. She hit me back and the fight was on. She began crying and I guess I was crying too and then, as suddenly as it began, it was all over, with my father standing between us, holding me at arm's length, looking amazed at us both.

"I thought the house was on fire when I came in just

now," he said. "Are you two all right, or do I send for the police?"

Jane was sobbing. I relaxed, and my father let go of me.

"OK," he said quietly, "let's have it, one at a time. Jane, you first."

"He hit me."

"She said I stole this glove."

"What glove?"

"This baseball glove. I found it in the park."

"Let's see it."

"It was lying in the grass."

"He was marking it up with my ink."

"I'll pay you back for the ink."

"Let me get this straight," my father said. "You found this glove in the park, brought it home, and then began marking it up."

I nodded.

"What did you do that for?"

"I . . . thought it'd be fun."

"Ball players don't mark up gloves."

"Thieves do," Jane said.

I jumped for her. My father caught me halfway. "Sit down."

I stood there.

"Sit down," my father repeated quietly but firmly. And I sat down.

"What reason do you have for saying what you just said, Jane?" my father asked.

Jane was silent.

"Jane," my father said, "you just accused Tim of stealing that glove. Do you *know* that he stole the glove?"

"No."

"Then why say that?"

"Why would he mark it up like that unless there was someone's name under those ink blotches?"

My father turned to me. "Was there a name on the glove?"

"No," I lied.

I had to lie. I wouldn't lie again—just one to get me out of this mess.

My father was silent for a moment. He looked at the glove. "Baseball gloves," he said, "especially good ones like this, aren't meant to be painted up. Fun with a glove is when you make a good catch with it."

He handed it back to me.

"There are several things we can do now to see that it gets back to its rightful owner, Tim. You can ask around school tomorrow while I ask out at the plant to see if anyone's boy left a glove at the park. If that doesn't work, we'll put an ad in the newspaper."

"But what about finders keepers, Dad? I've lost lots of things that nobody returned to me."

"You're not nobody. You're Tim Foster. And you'll make an effort to return that glove. Some boy may have worked a long time to earn enough money to buy it."

"Then he shouldn't have been careless enough to lose it."

"Carelessness isn't a crime—"

"Is finders keepers a crime?"

"It is when you don't make an effort to find the rightful owner."

"Dad, look at it this way. Most of the kids who go to Sampson School are rich kids. That's why they leave gloves like this around. They know they can always get another one."

My father smiled despite himself. He picked the glove up again and held it toward the light. For a second panic set in. Would he be able to see the boy's name through the ink? I held my breath. He finally turned the glove around. He wasn't looking for it. I know he wanted to believe me as badly as I wanted to own that glove. With it I'd have a chance to make a Little League team here. And he'd be proud of that. Dad was an old shortstop; he had played semi-pro ball in Illinois. I knew how much he wanted me to do well at baseball.

He turned the glove over in his big hands and then tossed it in my lap. "Tomorrow we'll both ask around. I'll also find some chemical cleaning agent that will take that ink off. Now I want you two to shake hands—"

"I won't shake hands with him," Jane said. "My shoulder's still sore where he hit me."

"You called me a crook."

My father sighed. "It's obvious that peacemaking only leads to another war. You go to your room, Tim. I've brought home some TV dinners tonight. I'll call you both in about a half hour."

After he left, Jane said: "Will you now kindly leave my room?"

"I'm sorry about hitting you."

"Forget about it. Just go."

"But I didn't steal the glove. I honestly found it in Sampson Park."

"I'm not interested. Please go."

"Don't you believe the truth?"

"I believe you, Tim. I'm just not interested anymore."

I felt like tears all over again. "You don't believe me, do you?"

"Tim, I believe you. Go wash your face. Here, if it makes you feel better, I'll shake hands with you."

It was silly, but she and I shook hands and it did make me feel better. I had no sooner got to the bathroom door than she called after me softly: "Tim?"

"Yes."

"I swear I won't tell Dad. Was there a name on that glove?"

For a split second I was tempted, but I didn't quite trust her. "No," I said.

"Good," she said, and ducked back into her room.

Did she believe me? I wasn't sure. But it didn't matter. The glove was mine. Any chemical thing Dad found to take off my ink designs would also take that boy's name off too. What was that name again? "Tad Myers"?

Well, tough luck, Tad Myers. Your loss is my gain. Finders keepers.

»2«

The Hazards of Soccer

Most of the bigger fifth graders at Sampson School are safety patrol boys. I was big but I wasn't one of those, for two reasons: one, I was new to the school and two, I wouldn't be a safety patrol boy even if they asked me. I think it's kid stuff to stand on a corner with a red belt and hold out your arms like a scarecrow. You have to do that in the rain too. And for what?

Every morning on my way down Granger Avenue to the school I went by two safety boys on corners. They'd stand there showing off with their hands outstretched, looking for cars. I just brushed right by them. The morning after I found the ball glove, I walked by the one at Granger and Baldwin.

"Hey," he said, "where do you think you're going?"

"To school. Where else?" I said.

"I can report you for that," he called after me.

"Go ahead. I don't care."

He couldn't report me because he didn't know my name. No one knew my name. Being a stranger in town had its good points as well as its bad.

Still, it didn't make sense getting in too much trouble with them so I avoided the second patrol boy by cutting through a backyard and into Sampson Park. Sampson School is at the north end of the park. In front of the school I could see a soccer game going on. This was the big deal before school started. I walked up to the game. They were all fifth and sixth graders.

"Any joiners?" I called out.

"The sides are all even," someone shouted, running by.

The ball got kicked toward me on the sidelines. I ran up to it and gave it a little kick and then kicked it again. I was in the game whether they liked it or not.

"Hey, whose side are you on?" a kid asked me.

"Not yours," I said, and gave the ball a good kick.

I didn't care which side I was on, and as the game continued I played on both sides. Sometimes I'd kick the ball toward one goal and sometimes to the other one. The kids got angry all right.

"Hey, who is that guy?"

"He's a new kid. No one knows his name."

They'll get to know my name all right, I thought, and kicked the ball again.

A figure loomed up, blocking my path. It was a little taller than me. Probably a sixth grader. "Hey, fella, what's your name?" he asked.

"Tim Foster," I said, a little pleased.

"Well, Foster," this kid said, "I've got a little advice for you. Want to hear it?"

"Sure," I said.

He beckoned me closer as if it was a secret. When I got next to him, he shoved me. I went over backwards, back over the kneeling form of another kid.

Everyone started laughing. I got up and went for the boy; he ducked under my fist, laughed, and ran off. I started to chase him but I was surrounded by a circle of kids, all laughing at me.

"I'll fight you all," I said, angrily.

I was so mad and they were laughing so hard that I didn't hear the bell ring or the teacher coming up.

"All right," she said, "the games are over. That was the second bell."

The circle broke up and everyone ran for the school. I didn't. I stood there, alone . . . except for one other kid about my size. He wore a blue warm-up jacket with some white patches sewed on it. The patches said: "Arborville Hockey Association." "Hat Trick Award." The kid was grinning at me.

"Do you want to fight too?" I said.

"About what?" he asked me.

I didn't know what to say. He laughed. "Come on, let's go to school."

I followed him. Kids were going into the school through the main and side doors, and there were safety patrol boys on each door. They greeted the boy in front of me.

"Hi, Tad."

"Hi."

Tad, I thought. Tad what? Could this be . . . Tad Myers? No, there were probably lots of Tads in Sampson School. Tad was a common name. And the kid who lost the glove might even had come from another school.

I went down the corridor. Everyone was greeting each other. No one said hello to me. My classroom was on the right and my teacher's name was Miss Stukey. She was young, not like the teachers we had back home, but she was a teacher just the same. Stuck with Stukey, I thought. I'd have to tell that to someone. It was pretty good. Stuck with Stukey.

Everyone in the classroom was in his seat except me. I was the last to enter and I still had park dirt on me from that trick the soccer players pulled on me.

I could see Tad in the third row. I hadn't remembered his being in the class but then again this was only my second day in Sampson School.

Miss Stukey looked down on me. "Good morning, Tim. Do you remember where your seat was?"

The whole class was looking at me. It was an old familiar sensation. All of them, and me.

I tried for a laugh. "My seat's right here," I said, patting my rear end.

There was a laugh, but not the kind I expected or wanted. It was small and sort of embarrassed and a little sneering.

"Your seat is in the front row, Tim. Please take it."

"Sure, I see it. My eyes aren't so good this morning."

"Ha, ha. He's a comedian," someone said.

I felt my face redden and looked around to see who the

smart aleck was. During recess I'd get even with him, but every boy in the class was grinning at me. I hated every last one of them.

We opened our geography books and the morning droned on.

When recess finally came we went outside into the park. The girls went off to the swings and to the cement walk for hopscotch and rope skipping. The boys started playing soccer. There were fifteen boys in the class and that meant seven on a side with one boy left out. I bet you know who was left out.

I stood there and watched them. Tad was the best player on the field, really well coordinated. He was fast too, and could dribble the ball down the field, poke it around a defender . . . always keeping it on his toe. I hate to admit it but I enjoyed watching him.

"Don't you play soccer, Tim?"

It was Miss Stukey.

"No, I play football and baseball."

"So do these boys. Would you like to get into the game?"

"Nah. Soccer's a kids' game."

"Have you ever tried it?"

"I don't have to. I can tell."

"Goal! Goal!"

"Good going, Tad."

"Way to go, Tad."

"It might interest you to know, Tim, that the boy who just kicked that goal—Tad Myers—is the best baseball player in the whole fifth grade."

I held my breath. So Tad *was* Tad Myers. It was his glove I'd found. I didn't know what to think. He had stayed after my scuffle with the other boys, maybe to help me. He'd acted friendly. He was a good ball player. And now I had his glove and had made it mine.

"I don't know how you can decide you don't like a game without ever having tried it. I'm going to ask Tad to put you—"

"Don't."

"Why not?"

"Please, Miss Stukey. I—"

"Kick it here, Kevin. Here, Kevin."

"All the way, Ralph."

The other team had the ball now and was attacking. A big kid with long dark hair was leading the way. He was good too, but not as fast as Tad Myers who had caught up with him. Tad was the only person between the boy and the goal. The boy went straight at Tad. Tad stepped to his right and then dodged left and got his foot on the ball and kicked it loose. The boy tried to turn, but he fell down. Tad had the ball now and he kicked it down the field. The flow of action went the other way and everyone was shouting for another goal when Miss Stukey blew her whistle.

"What'd she do that for?"

"Hey, Ralph's hurt."

"Ralph, you OK?"

"Did you kick Ralph, Tad?"

"No, he didn't kick him. He twisted his ankle."

"How's it feel, Ralph?"

"OK, I think."

"Get up slowly," Miss Stukey said. "There . . ."

"Ouch."

"You'd better rest on the side. I'm sure it's just a little sprain. Children, you've got only five more minutes."

"Can't we play more? We're only one goal behind."

"In forty seconds, you'll only have four minutes left."

"We're a man short."

"No, you're not. Tim Foster will take Ralph's place." Miss Stukey was very firm about it.

"Who's he?"

"The new kid, stupid," a boy said.

"We don't want him."

"Yes, you do," Miss Stukey said. "And while you argue you're just losing playing time."

"Do you know how to play, Foster?" someone asked me.

"Go ahead and kick the ball, Foster. Let's see if you know what you're doing."

Baby stuff, I thought. I gave the ball a good kick. It sailed over their heads.

"Hey, he's good."

"OK, let's play. Whose out is it?"

"Who had possession when Miss Stukey blew her whistle?"

"We did."

"No, you'd kicked it."

"But you hadn't touched it yet. We were the last ones to touch it."

"Tad, take it out."

After much discussion, Tad took the ball out. He kicked it to another kid who faked a kick at the faraway goal and then kicked it right back at him. I went in on Tad. He kicked it sideways once, twice, and then he kicked it right through my legs and caught up with it on the other side.

"Hey, neat."

"Way to go, Taddy boy."

Somebody on our team blocked a pass and now we had the ball. I ran down the sidelines.

"Wake up, Foster."

The ball went skidding by me.

"Tough luck," Tad Myers said.

"If he'd passed it right I'd have had it," I replied.

Tad glanced at me, but he didn't say anything. Someone on his team kicked it in from out of bounds, and then Tad had it and was dribbling down the field.

I was determined to make up for my mistake in missing the pass. Running alongside Myers, I bumped him off balance. Slightly illegal maybe, but it worked. I had the ball to myself. I decided to give it a good hard kick. My foot went back, and came around. Tad Myers tipped the ball away, too late for me to react. I was committed with all my might. My foot met empty air and, off balance, I fell down backwards.

That and Miss Stukey's whistle ended the game. Everyone was laughing, including Tad Myers. I jumped up and went for him. I shoved him, and he shoved me back.

The laughing stopped.

"Hit him, Tad."

"Give the sorehead a sock in the nose, Tad."

But Tad didn't do anything. His hands up, his eyes grave, he watched me closely.

"You think you're so good, don't you?" I said.

I shoved him again. He shoved back.

"Go ahead," I said. "Start something."

"You start," he said softly, "and I'll see what I can do about finishing it."

He meant it, I could tell. "OK," I said, "you asked for it."

"You're both asking for it," Miss Stukey said, stepping between us, "and as far as I'm concerned you'll both get it unless you stop right now. I'm sorry I encouraged you to enter the game, Tim Foster. I'll see you after class. And you also, Tad."

"Foster started it, Miss Stukey."

"It takes two to fight," Miss Stukey said.

"Not when Foster's around. All we were doing was laughing."

"I don't care what you were doing. Move along now. Recess is over. You also, Tim. Move along."

I was purposely lingering behind. The guys were giving me a lot of unfriendly looks and I didn't want any of them getting behind me. As soon as Miss Stukey got ahead of us, rounding up some more kids, the boy named Ralph came over to me, limping a little on his twisted ankle. He was bigger than me.

"You think you're pretty tough, don't you, Foster?"

"I'm not afraid of you, if that's what you mean."

"That's what I mean, OK. I'll fight you after school, bad ankle and all."

"Don't worry about that ankle. It'll be OK in five minutes."

"On second thought, I'll fight you right now." Ralph shoved me. I started to shove him back when this time Tad Myers came between us. "Cut it out, Ralph," he said.

"I can fight my own battles. Look, Foster, let's get something straight. No one's afraid of you or wants you to be afraid of him, so cut it out. I'll fight you anytime you want." Then he turned to Ralph. "Don't be a dope, Ralph, she'll end up keeping you after school and there's baseball practice today."

"She can't keep you too long, Tad," a boy named Howard said.

"I know, but in my case it doesn't really make any difference because I can't play today anyway."

"Why not?"

"I'm grounded from baseball till I find my glove."

"You lost your glove?"

"The Pete Rose model?"

"Where'd you lose it?"

Tad shook his head with a rueful grin. "I left it in the living room where my kid brother could get at it. He took it over to the park and left it there somewhere. My father and I went all over the park last night with a flashlight but we couldn't find it."

"Boy, that's tough."

"Your dad's mad, huh?"

"Very."

"If my kid brother ever did a thing like that, I'd—" Howard couldn't finish his sentence, so great was his imagined punishment.

Tad shrugged. "My brother says he'll pay me back if it's not found. He and I checked out his piggy bank this morning. He's got all of thirty-eight cents in it."

"Enough to buy a picture of a glove," someone said.

"Great."

"But, Tad, it's not your fault if your kid brother loses your glove."

"My dad says it is. If I'd put the glove away and so on and so forth."

"Is it just this practice he's keeping you out of?"

"Nope. All baseball till I find it."

"Oh, no," Howard said, "We can't win without you."

Ralph frowned. "Maybe someone found it. Did you have your name on it?"

"Yes."

"Then it'll turn up," Ralph said.

"But suppose no one returns it," a boy said. "Who'll pitch against Mario's on Saturday?"

"I can pitch," I said. They all turned to me, astonished. They'd forgotten about me.

"You," Howard said.

"Listen here, Foster," Ralph said, "you're the last guy we'd want on our team."

"We'd play eight men before we'd have you on our team," another boy added.

And still another said: "We'd rather have a pitcher with no arms than you."

"Even a girl."

I shrugged. I didn't get mad. There was no heart in their kidding. They were really worried about Tad Myers.

Tad looked at me. "I hope you can pitch better than you play soccer?"

"I never played soccer before in my life. Back home I used to pitch."

"Where's back home?" someone asked.

"Illinois."

"What'd you move here for?"

"My father —"

"What'd you play in? Little League?"

"Yes. I —"

"Regular or farm team?"

The questions came fast and furiously. At last they were beginning to notice me. It was baseball that broke the ice.

"I played regular." This would be my last lie.

"Maybe he ought to come to practice today."

"If that guy plays on our team," Ralph said, "I'm quitting."

"We need a pitcher, Ralph," Tad said.

"You're good enough."

"I'm really a shortstop and you know it. And we need at least two guys who can get the ball over the plate."

Ralph shrugged. "Oh . . . I don't care."

Howard said: "OK, Foster. We've got a practice at four o'clock at the diamond nearest the tennis courts. Mr. Herndon'll be there. He's our coach. We're the Warren Plumbers."

"The Warren Plumbers?" I couldn't help grinning.

"What's funny about that?"

"Nothing. It's just the first time I ever heard a baseball team called the plumbers."

"Foster, if you don't like it —"

"What was the name of your team back in Illinois?"

"The White Sox." That *had* to be my last lie. The White Sox were a major Little League; I'd played on the Mud Hens, a farm team.

"Well, we do things differently here. Mario's Supermarket could beat any of your Illinois teams and who ever heard of a team called a Supermarket?"

"Yeah, and your Illinois teams never had pitchers like Kearney Boylan or catchers like Casey Birdwell."

"Come on down to practice, Foster," Tad Myers said, "we need a pitcher. You already know most of the guys from class. Ralph Weyland is our first baseman, Charley Burns catches, Howard Kohn plays second, Kevin Reilly, Willie Warner, Paul Nisbet . . . some of the other guys are in other fifth-grade classes and a couple of fellows go to parochial schools. But none of them can pitch, so we're hoping you can."

"I'll be there." I couldn't get over his being friendly to me, especially after our near fight. To tell the truth it made me uneasy. I didn't really want him as a friend. Not while I had his glove.

"Hey, we'd better get going. Here comes Stukey."

Miss Stukey was bearing down on us like an express train. She must have thought we were fighting again. We all took off for school like a flight of sparrows. Even Ralph forgot to limp. I ran with the rest of them. It was only when we were inside the building and on the way to the classroom that something dawned on me.

How could I possibly bring my baseball glove to practice? Even with the ink designs, everyone would know right away whose glove it was.

I'd have to show up without a glove. Like Tad. Two pitchers without gloves. It was crazy. I had to figure a way out of this.

»3«

Baseball's Not for Liars

What's Mr. Herndon like?" I asked Tad Myers as we left school that afternoon. Miss Stukey only kept us a half hour and when she saw we weren't mad at each other, she just told us not to act like babies again and dismissed us.

"Well, he's strict," Tad said. "He knows his baseball and he doesn't like to clown around. I don't think he was ever a ball player himself, but he knows a lot. He says our age is the time you can develop good or bad habits. If he doesn't think you're hustling, you don't play."

"Will he let me join, do you think?"

"Sure. He'll have to contact the league president first. They don't let guys transfer from one team to another, but since you come from out of town, I think it'll be all right.

At least," Tad said with a grin, "I hope it'll be all right. We need another pitcher badly."

"Did you pitch last year?"

"Me and a guy named Shorty Calderon. Most of the time I'm a shortstop, and I pitch like one. Shorty was good though. He had great control and threw low pitches so they hit most everything on the ground. He moved away in December."

"What place did you guys finish in last year?"

"In fourth place. There're ten teams. The team that won the championship is the team we're playing Saturday morning in a practice game. Did you really pitch in Little League?"

I started to say: "Sure," but I stopped. I hadn't really pitched there. I'd pitched a few innings in the farm league. I decided to hedge on my answer.

"I know I can pitch, but I've only pitched a couple of innings at a time."

Tad laughed. "Well, you've got the confidence and Mr. Herndon says that's almost half the battle. There's the team."

We'd come round the hill and there were fifteen or sixteen boys in white uniforms throwing balls. They were having batting practice. A man with a clipboard was standing behind the pitcher's mound.

"How many guys are on the squad?"

"We try to carry about eighteen because someone's always going off to camp or summer vacation. We get down to about ten . . . and for a while last year we played with just nine guys. That was scary. Hello, Boomer."

A lanky kid playing center field turned around. He was

chewing gum and he had a devil-may-care expression about his eyes. Across his shirt were the words: WARREN PLUMBERS.

" 'Lo, Tad," he said, and spat.

"Boom, this is Tim Foster, new kid who's going to be on our team."

"Yeah?" Boomer looked me over doubtfully. "What's your position?"

"Pitcher."

"Yeah? Well, we need a pitcher because —"

"Look out!" Tad yelled.

A ball came out on a line right at Boomer's head. Boomer stuck his glove up and caught it.

"Next time, you won't have anyone to warn you, Boomer, and I'll get you." It was the coach, Mr. Herndon. He had thrown it. "This isn't a tea party. This is baseball. Anyone out of uniform, get off the field."

"That means us," Tad said, with a grin. "He's sore. Lotsa luck, Boom."

"Thanks for gettin' him mad."

"You're welcome."

The batter hit a ground ball down to second. Howard Kohn was playing second. He scooped it up and flipped it underhand to the first baseman, Ralph Weyland.

"Easy hop for you, Howard. Give me the bat, Randy."

Mr. Herndon took the bat.

"That's what he does at the beginning of the season," Tad said to me. "He combines batting and fielding prac- tice if he doesn't think a guy fielded right."

"Try this one."

Mr. Herndon hit a sizzler at Howard. Howard backed

off from it, knocked it down, and threw to first. In time,
I thought.

"Good recovery, but you could have caught it cleanly.
When you backed up you were letting the ball take charge
of you. Come in on it. You could have shorthopped it.
The instant that ball is hit, infield, you decide you're in
charge and not the other way around. Let's —"

He was about to give the bat back to the batter when
he saw the right fielder looking up at a jet trail in the sky.

Mr. Herndon slapped a fly ball at the guy. The right
fielder recovered in time, caught it, and threw it back in.
It was Paul Nisbet. He was grinning.

"That's one of Paul's tricks," Tad said, with a laugh,
"whenever he thinks he hasn't been getting enough business out in right field. He pretends he's bored, and not
paying attention, and he always gets Mr. H. to hit him
a fly ball. He's been doing that for two years now and Mr.
H. still hasn't caught onto it."

Mr. Herndon suddenly started batting balls around the
field. He hit a skidding grounder down the first baseline.
Ralph Weyland fielded it cleanly. Howard Kohn cut behind him to take the throw, but Mr. Herndon called out:
"Make the play yourself. You've got the time."

Ralph turned and ran and stepped on the bag. He
wheeled and whizzed the throw back to the catcher who
flipped it up to Mr. Herndon. The coach didn't catch it
but tapped it back onto the ground. The catcher jumped
out in front of the plate, picked up the ball and threw it
ten feet over the first baseman's head.

"Beautiful, Charley. You had your man by ten feet, now
you've got him on second."

"Just where I want him, Mr. Herndon. I'll pick him off second."

"Oh, you will, will you? Tippit, get out there and be a runner on second. We'll simulate this for a few minutes. Let's see if you guys can prevent Tippit from scoring."

Art Tippit who was in our class ran out to second. Mr. Herndon knocked a ground ball to third. Grabbing it, the third baseman motioned toward second, forcing Art Tippit back, and then threw to first. Tippit faked a run at third. Ralph fired the ball back to third and the third baseman caught it and glared at Tippit.

"Good play, Bobby," Mr. Herndon called out with a laugh.

"That's Bobby Herndon, Mr. Herndon's son," Tad informed me. "He's good."

Mr. Herndon cracked the next ball into left field on one bounce. Tippit came around third.

"Home," everyone yelled.

The throw came in wide and Tippit scored.

"All right, clean hit, fast runner, nothing to do about it. Let's get on with batting practice. Tom, you've got seven more swings. After Scopus, we'll go around the infield. Jeff, you'll spell Charley in a few minutes. Tippit, Green, Glazko, get out in the field. Let's keep the practice moving. We're using six balls, so look alert. Let them hit it, Kevin. Nothing fancy. For every guy who strikes out, I'll fine you a Dairy Queen."

"Do we get a Dairy Queen for every hit?"

"You get a smack in the rear for every good hit you don't get. Ten swings and run the last one out. We play him on the last one. Let's go."

A kid named Tom Scopus who couldn't hit at all was up. He swung feebly four times before he finally sent a dribbler down the first base line.

Then a pop up, and finally another dribbler this time down the third baseline. He was out by fifteen feet.

"Does Mr. Herndon have to play everyone?"

Tad grinned. "You don't think Scopus looks good." He laughed. "League rules say everyone up to the thirteen-year-old league has got to play at least one inning. Mr. Herndon plays everyone two innings and it makes problems. Scopus once struck out with the bases loaded in the seventh and us only a run behind. We lost, but Mr. Herndon thinks Tom is a slow grower, whatever that means."

"Not much when you want to win," I said.

"I know," Tad said. He cupped his hands around his mouth. "Come on, Ralph. Sock one out of here."

Almost in response to Tad's shout, Ralph Weyland smacked the first ball on a line into left field.

"Way to go," Tad shouted.

"Good hit, Ralph," someone called.

The next pitches were wide and then Ralph popped one up. While Ralph was taking his swings, Mr. Herndon came over to us. "I heard about your bad luck, Tad. I gather you haven't found it yet."

"No, sir."

"Well, I hope you do before Saturday's game against Mario's. C'mon, Randy, you can do better than that. Tired, Kevin? All right, Nisbet. Get in there and chuck." Mr. Herndon turned back to us. He was a short suntanned man with long sideburns. I couldn't quite picture him as a ball player. But his eyes were alive, roaming all over, even while he talked with us. I can remember my father saying good coaches had eyes in back of their heads.

"And I take it this is the new pitcher from Illinois."

"Yes, sir," I said.

"I'm Doug Herndon, the coach of this so-called baseball team. Nothing fancy, Paul. Lob them over. We can use a pitcher if you can really pitch. Can you?"

"I think so. I pitched some back home."

"Good hit, Howard. That's the way to meet it. Just take it easy. Stroke it. We'll save home-runs for the ball games. How old are you?"

"Eleven."

"When was your birthday?"

"February."

"All right. That makes you eligible for our league, though I'll have to file your name with the president. I'll get your address and other information later. You're bailing out of there, Howard. That ball won't hurt you. How many swings is that?"

"Three."

"Four," someone called out.

"One of them was high."

"You swung at it."

"Hey, a little less noise and a little more baseball," Mr. Herndon said. He turned to me. "OK, run home and come back in some baseball shoes or sneakers and we'll look you over."

I hesitated, and he saw me hesitate.

"What's the matter?"

How was I going to tell him I didn't have a glove I could safely bring to this practice, in front of this team?

Luckily, he was distracted by a bobble at second base.

"You didn't move your feet at all, Randy. You could have taken a step in and fielded that cleanly. C'mon now, my grandmother played ball better than you're playing right now. How does it feel out there, Paul?"

"Don't look any further for a pitcher, Mr. Herndon."

"Signed, sealed, and delivered," Mr. Herndon said, with a laugh. "What are you doing still here? I thought I told you to go home and change."

His voice was tough, but his eyes were friendly, and thus I was dismissed. "Howard, you're lunging," he shouted. "Just keep your eye on it. Every second. From the pitcher's hand to home plate. Don't anticipate. Just hit it when it reaches you. Hitting's the simplest thing in the world if you stop trying to think about it. It's eyes and wrists and putting it all together naturally. You told me you'd stop lunging and look at you now."

"That's the only way he has a chance to hit me," Paul Nisbet said, grinning.

Everyone laughed. Paul was throwing fat pitches up there and Howard waited on one, timed it, and hit it over second base.

"Now that's more like it. C'mon, Kevin. Move in on those. That's tall grass right now. The ball won't come to you on a silver platter. A smart runner would be on second right now. Move in a little, Boomer. Howard Kohn can't hit that far. As soon as Kohn is out, Tippit, come in and play third. Bobby, grab a bat. Haynes, you catch. Howard, run this one out. Foster, aren't you home and changed yet? Look, Son, if you're any good you'll make our team. If you're no good at all, you'll still make it. So get moving."

I had to laugh, despite my fears. Mr. Herndon was a pepper-pot, completely different from my quiet father. Dad was a ball player, Mr. Herndon was a coach. But Dad knew a lot of little things that only a ball player learned. Tiny things, like getting your elbow up a little at the plate, like where your left foot should come down in your pitching motion. Maybe Dad would want to help Mr. Herndon. Even though he didn't miss many things, Mr. Herndon looked like he needed help.

Howard swung and sent a grounder down to third base. Bobby Herndon scooped it up and whipped it across the diamond and Howard was out.

"Keep running," Mr. Herndon shouted. "Bobby, grab a bat. Move, move. Haynes, come in to catch. Paul, I'll catch till the equipment's ready. Give me your mask."

"Come on, Tim," Tad Myers said, "you'd better get going. I'll walk you home."

"You don't have to."

Tad Myers looked at me peculiarly. "Of course I don't have to," he said, and laughed. "You're a funny guy. I've got nothing else to do. Where do you live?"

"Pretty far from here."

He laughed again, as though I were a real comedian. "You couldn't live too far and still go to Sampson School. What street?"

In the worst way, I didn't want him to come to my house, but I didn't know how to stop him.

"Baldwin and Brooklyn."

"That's only four blocks away."

A crack of the bat turned us around. Bobby Herndon sent a deep fly into center. Boomer made an over the shoulder catch.

"He's good."

"Boomer's the best center fielder in the league. He, Paul, Willie Warner—he's the left fielder—and Ralph could play on any team in the league."

"What about you?"

He shrugged. "I play at it."

"Not according to Miss Stukey. According to her you're the best ball player in the whole fifth grade."

Tad blushed. "A lot she knows. If I'm so good, we should have beaten Mario's. In three years, we haven't won one game from them."

"Are they that good?"

"They've got a big pitcher named Kearney Boylan, and a hard-hitting catcher named Casey, and a shortstop . . . We can match the rest of them. You'll see for yourself Saturday morning."

"You think I can play Saturday?"

"I think Mr. Herndon wants to look you over first. If we don't find a pitcher, we'll finish last in the league. I'm not really a pitcher, but I can get the ball over. I know this sounds like bragging, but if I can't play, then we're really going to be sunk."

I didn't know what to say. If I could take back all my actions of the past twenty-four hours, the first would be bringing that glove home and making it my own. What was I going to do right now when Tad Myers came to my house? I didn't have a good glove. Somewhere, in some trunk or other, I had an old one from Illinois, but even last year it hadn't been any good.

"The only people who won't feel bad about my not playing are my folks." Tad shook his head. "My father thinks baseball is for the birds, and the schedule gives my mother indigestion. Two games a week when the season starts, and my brother's starting in the eight-year-old league and he's got one game a week. The supper schedule goes to pot, and it makes Mom mad. How does your mother feel about that?"

"My mother died last year. But she liked baseball a lot. My dad used to play semi-pro ball. We would go at night and see him play. Mom was a great fan."

"I'm sorry."

"It's OK."

For a moment neither of us said anything. Then Tad said: "You got any brothers and sisters?"

"An older sister. Her name's Jane."

"Is she nice?"

"She's terrible. Before Mom died she was OK. Now she thinks she's got to be my mother."

Tad smiled. "I hear older sisters are like that anyway."

"There's nothing worse than an older sister."

"Except maybe a kid brother who loses your glove. Boy, what a neat glove that was too. I'll never find another one like it."

I swallowed. "Maybe . . . you'll find it still."

"Not a chance. Some kid probably picked it up. He knew a good thing when he saw it, all right. By now, he's probably erased my name and put his own on."

Did he know? How could he say a thing like that? Had

he guessed? It was impossible. I'd have given anything in the world to be a thousand miles away from this spot.

But Tad went on. "And who can blame him? I don't know that I would have done any differently. It might be a poor kid who found it, a kid who didn't have a glove at all."

"I bet it turns up," I said, my voice sounding weak to my ears.

"I hope so too. Here's Brooklyn. Which is your house?"

"The little gray one over there. We're renting it."

"That's a neat house. And you've got a good driveway for basketball. We've got a good one too, but my mom won't let us put up a backboard on the garage because she says the ball will bounce into her garden. And my father won't argue with her because he doesn't want to be bothered."

"My dad'll put one up on our garage and you can come over here and shoot baskets. We had a backboard back in Illinois."

"Did you like it there?"

"It was great," I said, and immediately wondered why I said it. It hadn't been great at all. I'd never made the major Little Leagues, I hadn't any friends back there, Mom had died there and it had become a hard place to live. It wasn't half as nice as this town—I knew that right away. But I had got off on the wrong foot here, and I didn't know how to get back. So all I did was tell more lies, put more wrong feet forward.

We were in front of my house. "Look," I said, "you wait here. I'll be right out."

"OK," Tad said, and I knew he was puzzled as to why

I didn't ask him in. I was trying to remember if the glove
was downstairs or up. No, I'd left it up on my desk.

"Come on in," I said, "you can wait downstairs."

If my sudden change puzzled him, he didn't let on. We
went in. I could hear Jane moving around in the kitchen.

"Is that you, Tim?"

"Yes."

"What took you so long from school?"

I winked at Tad. "Oh . . . I walked home slowly. This
is Tad Myers, a friend of mine."

Jane stood in the doorway wearing an apron that had
flour all over it.

"Hello, Tad."

" 'Lo," Tad said.

"What are you making?"

"A chocolate cake. Are you in Tim's class, Tad?"

I closed my eyes. Here we go again . . . little mother
on the job.

"Yes," Tad said.

"Has he been in any fights yet? He was always getting
into trouble back home."

"Thanks," I said.

Tad grinned and winked at me. "No fights yet."

"I don't believe you," Jane said. "Tim always manages
to fight with people and then get them to stick up for
him. And I don't know why."

"Boy, I'm sure glad I brought a friend home. Now you
can see why I wanted you to wait outside, Tad."

Thank you, Sister.

I made for the stairs. "I'll be right down."

"I'll come up with you."

"No," I said quickly. "You stay down here. I'll be only a minute."

"His room's a mess," Jane said, "but it's the first time I've ever seen him ashamed of it. That's progress anyway. Nice to meet you, Tad."

"Same here," Tad said.

"And that's what an older sister's like," I called down the stairs.

"I heard that," Jane said from the kitchen.

My room was a mess. I hadn't made my bed or put things away, but it wasn't the condition of the room I was ashamed of. It was the glove sitting there in the middle of my desk with all those stupid ink designs on it. I picked up the glove and buried it into the bottom of my closet, below the shoes, socks, and games.

Close one, I thought. I changed my clothes, put on sneakers, and went back down the stairs. Tad wasn't in the hall. I heard his voice. He was in the kitchen talking with Jane.

A wave of panic hit me. Was she telling him more about me, and not just about the distant past, but about the near past like yesterday?

With thumping heart I listened by the door.

Jane was saying: "Dad says Tim could be a good athlete if he ever forgot about himself and how he looked and if boys liked him or not. He says that once Tim decides to play the game for its own sake, he'll help any team."

"Well, I hope he decides that," Tad says, "because our team needs all the help it can get. And maybe we can help Tim . . ."

Tad Myers had said that. He said it quietly and with friendship in his voice.

My eyes were teary. I wiped my nose.

"Hey, let's go," I called out.

Tad came into the hall and Jane came with him. "Where's your new glove?" she asked.

And there it was. Naked and terrible. Nothing could prevent all of it from coming out now.

"I —"

The phone rang.

"I'll get it," Jane said. "It's probably for me. Have a good practice, and remember, we're eating at six fifteen."

"Let's go," I said.

"Where is your glove?" Tad asked.

"We haven't unpacked all our things yet. I've got a new glove and I've got to oil it still. My dad won't let me use it before I rub some oil into it."

More lies. When was I going to be able to get out of this mess? And how was I going to be able to return Tad's glove to him? Because this was what I wanted to do more than anything else in the world.

"I'm sure you can borrow someone's glove for today," Tad said, as we walked back to the park.

»4«

Debut to Mixed Notices

"How many kinds of pitches can you throw, Foster?" Paul Nisbet asked me.

Paul was taking a breather on the sidelines. He was one of three black players on our team. Tad had told me that Paul was the team's most versatile ball player. He could play any position creditably.

"I guess I've got two or three pitches," I said. "I'm working on a curve."

"Hey, that's great. Foster's got a curve."

"I'm just working on it," I said nervously. Some place, somewhere, the lies had to stop.

"Don't ever let me catch you throwing a curve," said Mr. Herndon, coming up behind us. "Your arm's not ready for curves until you're fifteen years old. I've seen more youngsters with bad elbows just because they thought it would be cute to try throwing curve balls. All right, Foster, get out there and pitch. Nothing fancy. Just chuck it straight in there. I want to see if you've got an arm. Nisbet, you feed balls to him. Randy, move back to short. Kevin, to the outfield. Tippit, step out of the box, I want to let Foster warm up a bit."

The mound felt funny. It was a little higher than the one back home. And they were all watching me—Tad Myers from the sidelines, and the rest of them behind me. That felt funny too. I had borrowed Tippit's glove. Behind me, Paul Nisbet stood with a collection of balls at his feet. In front of me, Charley Burns squatted.

"Chuck easy, Foster," Charley Burns called out.

I decided my first pitch would probably be my most important pitch, if I were to make this team and thus make any friends. So I decided to put a little steam on it. It hummed in there, fast but high.

"Hey, how about that?" someone said.

"We got ourselves an arm, Mr. Herndon."

Charley Burns grinned. "One more like that and I go for a sponge."

Mr. Herndon frowned. "Take something off that pitch, Tim. Throw it up easy."

I ignored him. I liked the reaction I'd got. If they thought that one was hard, let them take a gander at this one. I kicked high and really burned one in there.

"Hey," Charley Burns said, and hopped about, holding his hand.

"All right," Mr. Herndon said, "give me the ball."

"What's the matter? What did I do wrong?"

"You don't hear well. You can sit down and watch practice until your hearing improves. When I told you to take something off it, you threw harder. I don't know about the team you played on before and how the coach ran it, but I'm the coach here and you do what I say or you don't play. Haynes, get in there and pitch. We'll only use one ball, Nisbet, so put the rest in the bag. Use the whitest one. We'll have a kind of game. Everyone runs out their hits. But the pitchers are lobbing them in. No strike outs. All right, Tippit, get in there. Let's get him out. Easy throws, Jeff."

I walked over to the sidelines, tossed the borrowed glove on the ground, and sat down. Tad Myers came over to me; he was grinning.

"You really get all mixed up, don't you?"

"What do you mean?"

"If he told you to throw fast you would have thrown slow, I bet."

"It's not that. I just wanted to show him I could really throw."

"Do you think you've got to throw hard for him to tell that? We've got guys who can throw as hard as you just threw and they're not pitchers. Boomer Gohane's got a tremendous arm, but he can't pitch. Mr. Herndon can tell whether you're a pitcher or not from a lot of little things, but when you do the opposite of what he says, he can tell you're not a ball player right away."

"Ah . . . forget it," I said.

Jeff Haynes was throwing fat outside pitches to Tippit. Mr. Herndon was calling balls and strikes from behind the mound. And Tippit had three balls on him.

"Put a little steam on it, Jeff," Mr. Herndon said.

Haynes threw it hard. It was right in there and Tippit popped it up.

"Does he pitch for you?"

"No. His arm gets tired after about twenty pitches. Jeff's our second string catcher. But Mr. Herndon's told him that as he grows and if he works with weights when he's older to strengthen his arms and neck, he could be a real good pitcher."

Bill Wilson was up next. Haynes threw up his blooper ball and Wilson hit a dribbler down the third base line. Bobby Herndon scooped it up and threw him out at first.

The third batter popped up after six pitches. Haynes looked to be reaching his limit. I saw Mr. Herndon glancing at me. Was he going to give me another chance? If so, I'd make the most of it. No more mistakes. No more trying to prove things.

The fourth batter took four balls and trotted to first. And that was the end of Jeff Haynes. Mr. Herndon left the mound and came toward Tad and me.

"Tad, did your father say anything about umping being forbidden?"

"No, sir," Tad said with a grin.

"All right then. Get out there behind the mound and call balls and strikes. Foster, are you ready for another shot at the mound?"

"Yes."

"Then get out there and pitch. Jeff, grab a bat."

"Oh, boy," Howard Kohn called out, "here comes the whizz kid again."

Nuts to you, I thought.

Tad tossed me the ball. "Don't blow it, Tim."

"I won't."

"Let him hit it. This is still batting practice even though we're making a play on the batter and the runners. I'm not keeping track of outs. Just balls and strikes. He wants to take a good look at you out there. See how you do under fire. So let them hit it."

"Don't worry about it, will you?"

"OK," Tad said. "Batter up," he called out.

Jeff Haynes stepped into the batter's box.

"Fat pitches all," Mr. Herndon called out.

If he misses this, he's blind, I thought. I tossed a fat one up there. The kind you'd throw to your baby sister. It was a little high and Haynes let it go but he took the opportunity to call out to me: "That's the kind of fat ones I like, old boy. Just a little lower."

"Forget him," Tad said.

"I have already."

Mr. Herndon knelt on one knee between third and home and watched me. I tossed another easy one up there. Haynes stepped into it and smacked it on a line over the shortstop's head. It wasn't that much over his head but the dumb guy mistimed his jump and he was coming down when the ball went over him. The left fielder tossed it into second.

"Nice hit, Jeff," the shortstop said to Haynes who was perched on first.

"Nice hit, baloney," I said. "If you'd timed your jump that would have been an easy out."

"Oh, come off it, Foster," the shortstop said.

"Play ball," Mr. Herndon snapped.

"Forget it, Tim," Tad Myers said. "Randy's doing the best he can out there."

But I couldn't forget it. It burned me up. It was one thing to make an error, even an error in judgment, but it was another thing to pretend the guy had got a clean hit. I was about to blow the ball past the next batter— Paul Nisbet—when I realized Mr. Herndon was watching me closely. How did I react to trouble? I let another nice fat one go up to the plate and Nisbet promptly banged it over the left fielder's head for a home run.

The shortstop called out to me: "Maybe if I timed that one I would have had that too."

"Ah, go stuff it," I muttered.

"Way to pound the old apple, Paul," Ralph Weyland called out from first. Another friend.

Willie Warner was up next. He grinned at me with a lot of teeth. "Got any more fat ones left, Foster?"

Nuts to you. To all of you, I thought. I reared back.

"Don't, Tim, don't," Tad said, warning me.

And nuts to you too.

I threw it as hard as I could.

"Look out!" Tad shouted.

It was a wild pitch, sailing right at Warner's head. He went down, and the ball just grazed his batting helmet.

I stood there shaken. Mr. Herndon was on his feet, looking toward me. Everyone else was looking at me too. Warner got up slowly.

"Nice going, Foster," Ralph Weyland said, "if they hit you, you hit them."

Warner spat deliberately out toward me. "Don't try that again, Foster."

Charley Burns tossed the ball back to me. "This is batting practice, Foster."

"Foster's too much of a big shot to pitch batting practice," Howard Kohn called out from second.

It really makes a guy feel good to have that kind of verbal support from his teammates.

Boomer Gohane called out from center: "Stick it in his other ear, Tim."

Old Boomer, I thought. Boomer was a ball player. Well, that's just what I'd do. The devil with all of them. And then as I wound up, I got the idea. Willie was waiting for another smoker. I gave him the big motion and spun it up soft and easy. Willie was way out ahead of the ball. He swung hard, missed, and fell down. I laughed in his face.

"I'll have that ball, Charley," Mr. Herndon said to the catcher.

He caught the ball and came out to the mound. His mouth was grim.

"What was wrong with that pitch, Mr. Herndon? It was soft and fat."

"It was a good game pitch but a poor batting practice pitch. Boomer, since you're so full of good advice about where to throw the ball, you get in here and pitch. Foster, I think you've got the arm but not the pitcher's temperament. Let's see what you look like in center field. Get out there."

So that was it. I'd had my chance.

I hesitated. I was tempted to chuck it all and go home, but Tad said softly: "Don't be a fool. Get out there and play center."

"OK," I said. "I've got nothing else to do anyway."

I went out to center field and as Boomer came in to pitch he winked at me. I didn't wink back. It was all right for Boomer to play the clown. He was an accepted member of the team. But I hadn't made it yet, and from the way I was going, it looked like I never would.

The exchange of positions between Boomer and me turned out to be a poor idea. Boomer couldn't get the ball over the plate and everyone complained about it. When he finally did, Willie Warner smacked it out toward me, high in the air. I took a step in, and as I did so, I knew it was a mistake. The ball was carrying over my head. I turned, and lunged. The ball fell a couple of feet beyond my glove. I went for it, booted it, finally picked it up. Willie was coming into third. I'd have to throw it home. The second baseman was calling for the ball, but they didn't know I could toss it all the way home. I didn't need him to relay a throw for me. I wound up and threw it as hard and as long as I could. The ball sailed way over Charley Burns' head and Willie Warner trotted home.

Mr. Herndon shouted at me. "You've got a cutoff man at second base waiting for that throw. Willie wouldn't have gone home if you'd thrown it to Howard. Use your head, Tim."

"I'm not an outfielder, Mr. Herndon. I'm a pitcher."

"You're neither. You're a Warren Plumber and that means you're a ball player. All right, let's get another batter in there."

I'd blown it at two positions and he'd just called me

a Warren Plumber. Then I'd made the team. I grinned, despite myself. This was a long way from the farm leagues in Illinois.

On the mound, Boomer found the range. He had absolutely nothing on the ball and the batters sprayed hits everywhere. I made one lucky catch but let another ball go through my legs. Mr. Herndon stopped play to demonstrate to me how an outfielder keeps a hard ground ball in front of him.

It seemed to me he was singling me out for criticism, though maybe I just didn't pay attention to what he said to the others.

Before Boomer got through everyone had batted except me. Mr. Herndon told me to come in and grab a bat.

"Move back the fences," Ralph Weyland called out. "Big stick."

"Should we put on an infield shift for Foster?"

"Clean up hitter. Look out below."

"Just meet the ball, Foster," Mr. Herndon said.

"I haven't had batting practice yet," I said.

"All right. We'll give Foster ten swings. You run the tenth one out."

"How do you like it, Tim?" Boomer called out.

"Anyway you do," I replied.

He grinned, shifting the chewing gum in his mouth and threw the hardest pitch I'd ever seen a kid throw. It was a foot over my head though. Everyone cheered and even Mr. Herndon smiled. "All right, Boomer, now be a pitcher."

"One of these days I'll control my smoke ball and then, you guys, watch out."

"One of these days we'll all be millionaires."

"Stop the gassing and throw the ball up."

Boomer threw in a fat one. I was so anxious to hit it out of the park that I missed it completely and almost fell down.

"Beautiful. A thing of beauty."

"Send him back to Illinois."

"They won't take him back."

"He's scared of you, Boom."

"Just meet the ball, Tim," Mr. Herndon said.

I popped up the next two pitches, getting under the ball, and finally I got solid wood on the ball and hit the fourth pitch into left field. Boomer threw two bad ones and then I popped one up to Willie Warner who was now playing third.

"C'mon, hot shot," Warner called out, "you can do better than that, can't you?"

You bet I can, I thought, I'll try and send one crashing into you. I tried to pull Boomer's next pitch down the third base line but I fouled it behind the plate and Charley Burns grabbed it.

Tad, who had stopped calling balls and strikes, shook his head. "Come on, Tim, relax up there."

Easy to say, hard to do, I thought, with so many guys wishing you bad luck. But I finally got hold of one and hit it on the ground between short and third.

"Hooray. Big stick is back."

I fouled off the next pitch and then Mr. Herndon told Tad to start calling balls and strikes again. I was to run if I hit it fair.

Boomer's first two pitches were wide. Then he threw a

fast one high. Three balls and no strikes. Should I take?
I looked at Mr. Herndon.

"Hit it if it's in there," he said.

Boomer winked at me and threw up his meat ball. I
stepped into it and smacked it safely into left center. It
was going between the outfielders. I made the turn at
first and headed toward second.

"Lucky rap," Ralph Weyland jeered.

Bobby Herndon, now playing left field, was just getting
to the ball. He was the regular third baseman. Even though
he had a good arm, it was an infielder's arm. Also he
might not know where I was, the way a guy who played
the outfield regularly would know. Chance for a triple. I
put on the steam and headed toward third. They were all
shouting "third" to Bobby. Willie Warner was blocking
the baseline, braced to receive the throw. I'd have to slide.
Come in hard. Show them. Show Mr. Herndon he had a
pitcher who could hit, run, and slide. Show Warner the
baseline belonged to the runner. Here we go, Willie. . . .

The ball and I arrived at the same moment. The ball
hit Warner's glove and I hit his legs. Willie went flying
up in the air. The ball was rolling around and I was on
third.

"Safe," Tad called out, "look out, Tim."

I looked up just in time to see a dark shape come flying
at me. It was Warner. I rolled over. He was on top of
me, punching away. I couldn't get out from under him.
His fists dug into my sides. And then suddenly he was
gone.

"Stop it, Tad," Mr. Herndon shouted.

Tad Myers had pulled Warner off and was swinging at him.

"Tad!" Mr. Herndon grabbed him and two boys grabbed Warner.

"Cool it, both of you. What is this? A boxing team or a baseball team?"

"He didn't have to jump on Foster when he was down."

"He spiked me."

"How could he spike you when he's wearing sneakers?"

"Well, he hit me when he came in."

"You were blocking the baseline. He had every right to slide into you. Didn't he, Mr. Herndon?"

"Yes, he did," Mr. Herndon said, "but I'll go along with Willie on this one. I thought Tim gave it a little extra for a practice." He looked at me and then at Willie and I knew he was unsure how to handle this. I had done the right thing as far as baseball went. I had as much right to that baseline as Willie, and Willie, instead of shaking it off, had jumped on me. They were all on Willie's side except for Tad. I could guess what else Mr. Herndon was thinking: his team was fighting each other instead of helping each other and maybe this new kid Foster was a rotten apple that spoiled things.

At that moment I just felt weak and tired. I wasn't mad at anyone. I wished I'd never tried out for this team. I was sure Mr. Herndon was looking for a graceful way to get rid of me.

"Are you all right, Foster?"

"Yes, sir."

"Then get on your feet. As for the rest of you, this seems

to be a good time to call a halt to this circus. Bobby, you and Kevin get the equipment together and put it in my car. Paul, give them a hand. We'll have an intra-squad practice game tomorrow at four-thirty right here. All of you show up or we won't have enough for two teams. Foster will pitch for one team and, Tad—you think you'll be able to play tomorrow?"

Tad shrugged. "I don't know. It depends on my father and if I find that glove."

"Well, if you're able to play, you'll pitch for the other squad. Otherwise, it'll be Jeff to start. I thought this practice today had its good moments as well as its lousy ones. Some of you hit the ball pretty good, and made some good plays in the field. But it ended in a fight. A stupid fight with only one man fighting. Willie, if you're going to be a ball player, you'll have to learn a few things. Don't carry grudges. You make a fool of yourself and a loser out of your team when you carry a grudge. You could have put the tag on Foster without blocking the baseline, but you wanted to get even with him for decking you at the plate. That's a silly way to play. Baseball's a skill game; you've got to keep your cool. Get mad in football, and you might win. Get mad in baseball, and you fall apart. Saturday morning we play Mario's Supermarket. We haven't beaten them in three years. How are we going to beat them if we're fighting among ourselves. All right, I want you two guys to shake hands."

"I won't shake with him," Willie said.

"Willie," Mr. Herndon said softly, "you either shake hands with Foster or you're off the team."

There was a silence. Everyone looked at Willie Warner. His face was red. He had all those teeth showing. He was supposed to be a good ball player but he looked like a farm kid to me.

"Oh, go ahead," Ralph Weyland said. "You can keep your fingers crossed so it won't mean anything."

The other guys laughed. Willie grinned. "OK," he said. He came up to me and stuck out his hand.

We shook hands. I looked at his left hand. His fingers were crossed.

What he didn't know was—mine were too.

"Practice tomorrow, four-thirty," Mr. Herndon said grimly. "And tomorrow, let's play baseball."

So ended my debut as a member of the Warren Plumbers. It was not an altogether happy one.

»5«

Good-bye to Designs

"This is the best cake you've ever made, Jane," my father said.

"Thanks," Jane said. "For once something I learned in school paid off."

"Lots of things you learn in school will pay off, Jane. Not as quickly as a recipe maybe, but they'll last longer. Tim, I asked around the shop but no one seems to have a son who lost a glove. Did you have any luck at school?"

"No," I lied.

"Well then, our next step is to put an ad in the paper. And also get rid of those ink designs. I bought some ink eradicator, Tim. It's on the coffee table. I want you to go to work on the glove."

"I will, but—"

"But what?"

"I was wondering . . . Dad, I made the baseball team. The Warren Plumbers."

Dad's face creased into a real smile. He rarely smiled anymore. Jane nodded, pleased.

"Why, Tim, that's wonderful. Congratulations."

"It's not so great as that. Anyone can make the team really, but it looks like I'll be a pitcher. They want me to pitch a couple of innings in an intra-squad game tomorrow."

"Is that right? Tim, that's terrific."

"And Saturday we've got a practice game against last year's champs—Mario's Supermarket."

"Why that's fine. But you sound like you've got something else on your mind."

"I do."

"Fire away."

"I need a new glove."

My father's face was a blank. "You mean, that little old glove you used back home isn't good enough for Michigan?"

"Dad—"

But he was grinning, and I knew it was all right.

"And I bet you want a glove just like the one you found."

"Well, it doesn't have to be exactly like it . . ."

"Do you know how much that glove you found costs?"

"Twenty dollars."

"At least."

"Suppose no one claims it," Jane said.

"Then Tim can keep it," my father said. "And you might as well play with it till someone claims it."

The point was: I couldn't play with it, but I couldn't tell them that.

"I'll have to get a new glove sooner or later, so why don't we go out tonight and get one? I've got ten dollars I can chip in."

"That's silly, Tim. You can use the one you found till—"

"But suppose I hurt it or something."

"Now how are you going to do that? That's a good glove."

"But, Dad—"

I know that I looked unreasonable in their eyes; the fact was that I felt unreasonable. But I'd have to have a glove of my own in practice tomorrow, and if I dug up that old glove from Illinois, I'd make a fool of myself.

"Tim," my father said, "I was planning to work on the downstairs bathroom . . . getting it ready for painting. Isn't it silly to go dashing off looking for a glove when you can use one temporarily?"

"Aw, Dad . . . please."

He didn't know what to make of it and since I couldn't explain it, we all sat there silently. Finally my father said: "I guess you're pretty excited about this ball team of yours."

"I am."

The answer pleased him. "And you're beginning to like it up here a little, aren't you, Tim?"

"A whole lot."

He wanted to find a reason to take me out now to buy a new glove.

"Tim even brought a friend home today. A nice kid named Tad Myers."

"Is he in your class?"

"Yes."

"And I suppose he's got a great baseball glove too?"

I nodded.

"Well, all right. Get your money and put a jacket on and I'll meet you in the car. We'll go down to the Sports Mart on West Stadium. When we get back though, you'll have to go to work on that old glove. I want those designs off tonight. I'm to put an ad in the paper tomorrow. The ink eradicator is in the living room."

"Thanks, Dad. I'll get those designs off."

"What's your coach like?" Dad asked me, as we drove toward the Sports Mart.

"He seems pretty good. He's a little guy and talks a lot and he doesn't have any help."

My father glanced at me amused. "Now what's that supposed to mean?"

I shrugged. "Nothing, except one adult and eighteen kids is a lot."

"And you told him your father could help."

"Oh, no. But I was thinking it."

"Get that thought out of your mind, Tim. We've still got a lot of settling in to do."

"Do you remember back home, you said you were going to help coach in the Little League?"

"Yes."

"And then Mom got sick . . . and . . ."

Neither of us said anything.

"You stopped everything."

"No, Tim," my father said gently, "everything stopped itself."

"But now. . . Now it's different. And Mr. Herndon is a nice guy and he knows a lot about baseball, but he never really played it himself, and there's lots of things you've told me that these guys need telling, too. And Mr. Herndon just doesn't know everything."

"You're very persuasive, Tim."

"Will you help, Dad?"

"How do you know he wants help?"

"I don't, I guess. But I could ask him."

Dad laughed. "You'd better let me ask him. So you want to get your old man back in a ball park. Well, maybe it's not such a bad idea. You've got me out to the Sports Mart and now you're working on me to coach. Tim, you'll end up a politician."

"Not with my temper."

"Have you been having trouble here already?"

I hadn't meant him to ask that. I was just being honest. Well, I'd have to go on being honest.

"A little."

"In school?"

"Yes. And at practice today. But I'm over it now and I'm going to try not to let it happen again."

"Good for you. Do you want to talk about it?"

"No, if it's OK with you."

"It's OK with me."

We went into the Sports Mart. There were lots of gloves around, even the Pete Rose model that Tad had lost. But

I'd better not get that. There was another glove that felt just as good, an Al Kaline model. Dad examined it.

"The most important thing is how it feels to you," he said.

"It feels good. Stiff, but good."

"All new gloves feel stiff. Examine the webbing. Does it look well sewn? How about the padding? You can always take padding out but it's harder to put it in. On the other hand you don't want too much padding. You want to get the feel of the ball through the leather. But you don't want any broken bones either. How does it feel?"

"I like it."

So we bought the Al Kaline model and Dad wanted to know if I needed any baseballs.

Baseballs? We had just one brown one home. So Dad bought two new baseballs, the most expensive ones. And then he bought some breaking-in glove oil.

"That's the trouble with spending money. It gets to be fun." He grinned. "I don't know much about this oil, but let's give it a try."

"What kind of oil did you use?"

"A special mixture. Vinegar, linseed oil, and spit. In equal proportions. You're going to take care of that glove, now, aren't you, Tim?"

"Oh, yes."

"Put some of that oil in there and rub it in, firmly and steadily and evenly. Do it tonight and every day. Tonight stick a ball in the pocket and tie the glove around. That way you'll get a start on a pocket. Next week, I'll see if I can get home a little early and you can pitch to me."

"We don't have a catcher's glove."

Dad laughed. "So you think I need a catcher's glove to catch you?"

"I hope so."

"Well, we'll see. And don't forget about getting those crazy designs off the glove you've found. I want to put an ad in tomorrow's paper."

"Dad, could you hold up on that? I didn't get to ask every kid in class. Give me one more day."

"All right. But go to work on those designs right away."

I did. As soon as we got home, I oiled my new glove and tied it around a ball. Then I went to work on Tad's glove. Opening the ink eradicator, I put some on a rag, and started on the back of the glove first. I wiped gently and the ink designs began to come off. The trouble was that it left the leather a little lighter where the ink had been. I took the glove downstairs and showed the light spot to my father.

"I thought that might happen. I don't think it'll hurt the glove though. When you're done we can put some stain or shoe polish on the light spots."

I went back upstairs and worked on the rest of the designs. Jane brought some shoe polish in.

"Do you think shoe polish will hurt it?" I said.

"Don't be silly. Shoes are made of leather. Besides, Dad says to use it."

"All right, but I'm not ready yet." It took me at least a half hour before I got around to the crucial part of the glove. Maybe if I rubbed lightly, my ink would come off but Tad's older ink would stay on. What if both came off? How would Tad even know it was his glove? And what would he think if he knew it was his? That someone had stolen his glove, erased his name, and then decided to "lose" it again.

The first thing was to see if I could take off the ink block without the name.

I got a new piece of rag soaked it in the ink eradicator and rubbed gently, very gently. It was slowing things up but it gave me, I thought, a fighting chance.

As it turned out, there was no chance at all. I worked for about fifteen minutes on that one spot and when I was done, everything had come off.

Now what?

"Tim," my father said, "it's after nine o'clock. Let's see how you're doing."

He came up into my room and picked up the glove. Then I realized how lucky I was that Tad's name had come off.

"Well, you did a good job. When this dries put some shoe polish on it. Don't use too much. Rub it in with a paper towel. How's *your* glove?"

"I'm trying to make a pocket. Can I use it tomorrow?"

"Of course you can. The more work it gets the better."

"Dad, thanks."

He looked at me. "Tim, I'm happy you made the team, happy you're making friends and liking it here. You don't have to be a baseball player, as far as I'm concerned. Playing ball is fun, but there are more important things in life. Twenty more minutes and then wash up for bed."

While the ink eradicator dried, I worked on my glove, squirting some more store-bought oil into it and spitting into it for good measure. It smelled good. All new and leathery and oily.

Finally I was ready to rub shoe polish into Tad's glove, a little at a time, mixing spit with it, so that it would match the original color. It didn't match exactly, but Tad could always think that the dew or something had got to it.

Then I got the bright idea of rubbing polish and spit over the rest of the glove. It looked good; the light band around the top was gone.

Only one thing would Tad notice: his name wasn't there. The only thing I could do was to forge his name back onto the glove. But I couldn't remember how he'd written it.

He might not know I'd stolen the glove, but it would probably always puzzle him, and he might bring it up again and again. And maybe just once he'd bring it up in this house and Jane would say: "But that's the glove Tim found and put ink designs on and so forth."

What if Tad had signed it in script? I couldn't imitate his handwriting unless I found his signature and practiced copying it. All that would take time, and Tad wouldn't get to play in either of the games coming up unless he had his glove back.

What I ought to do was take a chance he'd printed it. And then another idea hit me and I went into Jane's room to look at her clock.

"Aren't you in bed yet?" Jane said, which is just the kind of question an older sister asks you when you're walking around with all your clothes on.

"Yes, I'm in bed and fast asleep," I said.

"Don't be smart," she said, "and don't make Dad come upstairs to put you to bed. He's done enough for you tonight."

"I have to call someone on the phone, and then I'll go right to bed."

"Whom do you have to call at this hour?"

"Someone."

Before she could pile on with more questions, I went into Dad's room where the extension phone was. I looked up Myers in the phone book and found one on Lincoln Avenue which was near here. I hoped he wasn't asleep.

A lady answered.

"Is this the Myers'?" I asked.

"Yes."

"Is Tad there?"

"Tad's gone to bed."

"Oh."

"Who's calling?"

"Tim Foster."

"Oh, yes. You're the new boy. Well, he's just gone to bed. If it's important I can get him up."

"I guess . . . it's not important."

It was the most important thing in the world, but I couldn't tell her that.

"Wait a second, Tim. I think he's up anyway. It's for you, Tad, but please don't make it long."

Tad got on.

"This is Tim. I just got a new glove."

"Huh?" Tad said. "Is that what you called me about?"

"Well, yes. I mean, I don't know how to break it in."

"You said your dad was an old ball player."

"He was. But he's not home now. What kind of oil do you use?"

"I buy the oil at the store. It's for breaking in gloves."

"Do you think I ought to write my name on the glove?"

"It won't make any difference," Tad said, bitterly. "Someone will take it even if your name is on it."

"Did you have your name on your glove?"

"Yes, and a fat lot of good it did me."

"Maybe the person who found your glove couldn't read your handwriting."

"They could read it all right," Tad said, "because I printed my name in capital letters. Even a kindergarten kid could read it."

"What kind of ink did you use?"

"How do I remember? Maybe it was black ink. But, Tim, you don't have to do what I did. Remember, I ended up losing my glove."

"You can't tell, Tad. Someone may still find it."

"I'm sure somebody has already. Tim, my mom's giving me a dirty look. I've got to go now. What kind of glove is it?"

"It's an Al Kaline model."

"Great. Bring it to class tomorrow. We can look at it during recess."

"I will. Good night, Tad."

"Good night, Tim."

I hung up, excited. He'd printed his name in capital letters and with black ink probably. I could borrow Jane's ink again, and I knew how to make neat capital letters.

"Hey, can I borrow your pen and black ink?" I asked Jane.

"Dad's going to be mad."

"I just want to write my name on my glove."

"Take it, but hurry."

I took her ink into my room.

"Tim," my father called up the stairs, "are you ready for bed?"

"Just about there, Dad."

"If you're not in bed in ten minutes, Tim, I'm going to be very sorry I bought you that glove."

"I'll be in bed, Dad."

Carefully, I printed Tad's name in capital letters in about the same spot it had been. Then I rubbed a little more shoe polish over his name so it looked faded. Perfect. It looked just right.

I gave the shoe polish back to Jane and was about to hop into bed when I realized my father could come up and spot Tad's glove. I shoved it under the bed. Then I lay down again and pulled the covers up.

I had a glove. By tomorrow Tad would have his glove back. All I had to figure out now was a way to get it back to him without letting him know who had taken it.

I thought and I thought . . . and then an idea came to me. I got up and walked into Jane's room.

"Now what is it?" she asked.

"Could you wake me up when you get up?"

"You don't have to be in school till eight thirty."

"I know, but I've got to meet someone before school starts."

"All right, I'll wake you when I get up."

"Tim," came a quiet warning call from my father.

"Good night, Dad."

"Good night, Tim."

"Good night, Jane."

"Good *night*," she said, exasperated.

I went to bed grinning. Everything, I thought, was going to be all right.

»6«

Another Play Fouled

It was a simple plan and I thought it a good one. I'd put
Tad's glove in a paper bag and hide it at the base of a tree
in the park. Then during recess I'd play catch with Tad,
throw the ball over his head toward the tree, run after it
with him and get him to look in the bag.

School starts at eight thirty, but kids come as early as
eight o'clock because they play soccer in front of the school.
When I got there at ten minutes to eight that morning there
were only one or two people around, and they didn't notice
me. I put the paper bag at the base of an oak tree, about two
hundred yards away from the school. Scuffing it up a little
to make it look like some hasty picnicker had left a half-
eaten lunch behind, I threw some cut grass on top and it
began to look like litter. My only worry then was that the

groundskeeper might pick it up, but he was working at the far end of the park and I knew I was safe.

Then I sauntered toward the school. I had my glove and a ball with me and a math book. By the time I got to the play area there were a dozen kids. We threw my ball around till someone arrived with a soccer ball.

Tad and the other kids joined the game late, and I pointed to my new glove.

"I'll look it over during recess," he said.

The minute we got outside I showed everyone my new glove. Ralph Weyland was hanging around with his usual smirk. He carried his jacket rolled up in his hand, swinging it back and forth. I ignored him and gave my glove to Tad who pounded it.

"Feels good. Just the right amount of padding."

"Here," I said, "I'll toss you some."

"I'll toss *you* some, it's your glove."

"You find your glove yet, Tad?" Howard Kohn asked.

"Nope."

"Go over there," I said, "I'll throw them easy."

"This is silly," Tad said, "I should be throwing them to you."

"Will you be able to play today?" Howard asked.

"Not till I find my glove," Tad said.

"Go ahead," I said. "Move out."

Tad looked puzzled. "It's your new glove, Tim," he said.

"Keep going," I said. "I can peg this ball hard at a hundred feet."

"Foster, you'll never win any prizes for modesty," Howard Kohn said.

I was aware that Ralph Weyland was eyeing me curiously, swinging that rolled up jacket of his.

Bobby Herndon came up. "What gives?"

"Foster's bragging how far he can throw a ball."

"Further than you, Howard," I said.

Tad, puzzled as to why he was using my glove and not me, was about sixty feet away. He wasn't going to back up any further, so it was now or never. The oak tree was about two hundred feet away. It would take a good long throw to get near it, and it would look funny throwing it two hundred feet when Tad was only sixty feet away, but if I could get Ralph Weyland or Howard Kohn into a throwing contest . . .

"I bet I can throw this ball further than any of you guys."

"How much do you want to bet?" Ralph asked.

"A dime."

"Throw it," Ralph said.

"Back up," I shouted to Tad, "I'm going to throw it as long as I can."

"It's a bet," Howard said.

Tad backed up, looking doubtful about the whole thing. I stepped forward and threw it long and high toward the oak tree. It was a good throw and rolled within six feet of the tree.

I turned to Ralph who was looking at me strangely. "Let's go mark the spot," I said, and before he or any of the others could say anything, I ran ahead.

Trotting after the ball and shaking his head, Tad was surprised when I came up alongside him.

We were about twenty feet from the bag and ball

DENVER
PUBLIC LIBRARY

SEP 1971

CITY & COUNTY OF DENVER

"Hey, Tad, grab that paper bag and we'll use it to mark the spot."

"Nope," Tad said, and tossed me my glove. "I'm not getting mixed up in any silly throwing contests. Who's got a soccer ball?"

"Get the bag, Tad," I said, desperately. The others had caught up with us, Howard, Bobby, and Ralph.

"Nope," Tad said, "you get it yourself."

It wasn't the way I wanted it to happen, but it was the only thing I could do. "All right," I said, "I'll get the bag." I walked over to the brown bag. "Looks like someone left their lunch here," I said. "Hey, Tad, Howard, any of you guys short a sandwich?"

"Maybe you are," Ralph Weyland said, "open it up and see if it's ham or cheese."

I grinned. "I will," I said.

The moment I touched the bag I knew something was wrong. I picked it up. It was as light as a feather. There was nothing inside.

The glove was gone.

I felt sick.

"Well, what was it?" Ralph Weyland asked with a sneer. "Ham or cheese? Or was it something else you were looking for?"

Everyone looked at Ralph, amazed. I did too.

"Was it this you were looking for, Foster?" Ralph unrolled his jacket and held out Tad's glove.

"Hey," Tad said, "that's my glove. My glove! Where'd you find it, Ralph?"

Everyone crowded around Ralph except me.

"I found it in that paper bag," Ralph said. "The paper bag that Foster's holding right now."

They turned to me and looked at the bag.

Tad gave a puzzled grin. "You found it in that bag. Hey, what's going on?"

"Foster knows, don't you, Foster?"

I didn't say anything. I was trapped. They were all looking at me.

"Tim," Tad said, uneasily, "what's it all about?"

"If Foster won't tell you, I will," Ralph said. "I had to come to school early to clean the erasers. I was cutting across the park when I saw Foster hanging around this tree. I thought he was digging up something. I got curious and waited till he left. Then I circled over and investigated. There was this bag. I gave it a kick, and then I opened it up and saw your glove in it. Foster had put it there."

Tad turned to me, baffled. "Is that true, Tim?"

"Sure it's true, Tad," Ralph said. "I saw it with my own eyes."

"I'm asking Tim. Is that true? Did you put my glove there?"

I could lie. It would be my word against Ralph's. No one else had seen me.

I looked at their faces: Ralph, Howard, Willie Warner, Bobby Herndon, two or three others . . . And then I looked at Tad. He wanted to believe me. I knew that. He wanted us to be friends. He'd take my word over Ralph's. All I had to say was "No, I didn't put the glove there."

I said: "Yes. I put it there."

There was a silence.

Tad was stunned.

"Look, I can explain—" I began.

"What's there to explain?" Ralph sneered. "You're a crook. That's all the explanation we need. I thought there was something phony about you from the start."

For an instant my hands lumped in anger, but I forced them to unclench. What good would it do to hit Ralph, to hit anyone? I wanted to explain to Tad. I had made a mistake. Now, I just wanted to get back on the right track. Wouldn't they let me do that?

"Come on, Tad," Ralph said. "He's yellow as well as a crook. Let's go back and play some soccer. Come on, guys."

They walked away from me as though I had a disease. I stood there for a moment, and then I heard Miss Stukey blowing her whistle. Recess was over.

Everyone ran to the building, everyone except me.

I couldn't go back to class. The word would be out. I could hear Ralph and Howard telling the other kids right now.

"Hey, did you hear what Foster did?"

"Miss Stukey, Tad's got his glove back, and you know who had it?"

I turned and ran. It was stupid and foolish, but it was all I could think to do. I ran home. I could dimly hear Miss Stukey's whistle, but I paid no attention. I wasn't going back —not ever.

When I got home, I threw myself on the couch in the living room, and then it came. I don't know at what age boys aren't supposed to cry anymore but I started crying. I wept for my mother, for my father . . . for myself. I don't know how long it was before I fell asleep . . . but when I woke up my father was sitting there.

"Good snooze, Tim?" Dad asked me quietly.

I sat up and shook my head. My face felt dry and salty. Dad handed me a comb. "Wash up and comb your hair."

"What time is it?"

"Twelve noon."

"What are you doing here?"

"Your teacher called me at work. Go wash up and then we'll talk about it."

I looked at him closely to see if he was mad or not but his face held no expression at all. When I got back Dad was in the kitchen. He had a carton of milk out and was making cheese sandwiches for us both. I waited for him to start asking me what had happened, but the first thing he said was:

"Mayonnaise or mustard on your cheese?"

"Mayonnaise."

He spread some on and cut my sandwich, then he cut his, and we both sat down and ate. I felt starved. I could have eaten about ten cheese sandwiches.

Dad smiled. "Nothing like a sprint away from school to give a guy an appetite."

I grinned, embarrassed. "I'm sorry."

"I am too. Want to talk about it?"

"No, but I guess I have to."

"I guess you do."

"It's not what you think."

"How do you know what I think?"

"You think it's got to do with school."

"Why don't you tell what it has to do with?"

"I . . . don't know where to begin."

"At the beginning."

"You're going to be mad at me."

"Maybe . . . maybe not. Why don't you start?"

I hesitated. I looked at Dad, at his lean face, full of wrinkles caused by the worries of a young man bringing up two kids without a wife. He was a quiet man, my father, an athlete, sure of himself, and self-contained. I was always a little afraid of him, but I guess more than anything else in the world I wanted him to approve of me. The way I wanted Tad to approve of me. Well, it was all over with Tad, but I still had a chance with my father. . . .

I took a deep breath and I told him the whole story during which I admitted how I'd lied—to Tad, to Jane, to him . . . to just about everyone.

"But I was only trying to make things right again, Dad. And they wouldn't let me. They were all against me and were telling everyone including the teacher that I'd stolen the glove. I couldn't face going back to class, so I came home. I ran home and I guess . . . I cried and fell asleep."

I couldn't meet his eyes. After I was finished, I sat there, and he sat there, looking at me, but not saying anything. Then he said:

"Do you want some cake for dessert?"

"Aren't you mad at me?"

He shook his head. "No."

"But I did wrong."

"Yes, you did. But you already know it in a way I could never tell you with words. Lies never got anyone anywhere, Tim. They always come home to trip you up. But that's all over. Now the question is: where do you go from here?"

"I can't go back to school."

"Why not?"

"I can't face them."

"Can't you?"

"Dad, don't make me go back to school."

"It's a coward's way out to hide in here, Tim."

"I don't want to go back to that school, Dad. I hate it there. I hate this town. Why can't we go back to Illinois? Or somewhere else?"

"How about a little cave in Wyoming somewhere where no one would see you?"

"Dad, please . . ."

"Running away is no good, Tim. You know that."

"I couldn't face those kids, Dad."

"Why don't you tell Tad and the others everything you told me? How you tried to get it back."

"They wouldn't listen. They wouldn't believe me."

"How do you know?"

"I know."

"All right, suppose they don't. So what? *You* know what the truth is. That's all that matters. I know it'll be hard, Tim. I've got an idea what you're going through. You're not the first person who told lies and got caught. I used to tell quite a few myself when I was a kid."

"I don't believe you. You're just trying to make me feel better."

My father laughed. "No, I'm not. I'm just telling the truth. The point is, Tim—you have to take what comes now. That's the other side of the coin. You'll go back to school and you'll take it and it's as simple and as tough as that. And you'll bounce back, because you've got good stuff in you. You'll do your school work and you'll play in your game too."

"Oh, I'm sure I'll be kicked off the baseball team, Dad."

"How do you know that?"

"They won't want me on the team, they said so."

"I see. And do they run the team or does Mr. Herndon?"

"They won't play if I'm on the team. I just know that."

"That sounds like you think they're running the team. Tim, let's take things one at a time. You go back to school and after school—what time's practice?"

"Four thirty."

"You go to practice then."

"Dad, I'll go back to school, but please don't make me go to baseball practice."

"Scared, Tim?"

"Dad . . ."

"You'll take your lumps in the classroom and on the ball field and you'll come back because you're my son and because I know you can do it. Tim, there's something we've never talked about because maybe it wasn't necessary, and maybe it still isn't. But . . . you're growing up without a mother. It's not easy for you, it's not easy for any of us. We're all going to make mistakes, but we're in this together, the good as well as the bad, and when we make a mistake, we bounce back. Right?"

He put a hand on my shoulder. I nodded, and then I came into his arms and we held each other tight.

I knew then that Dad needed me as much as I needed him. I knew too that we'd bounce back, both of us.

I went back to school that afternoon.

»7«

A Team Divided

In one way it was good that most of the guys on the team were also in my class. That way I was able to face the class and the team at the same time.

I got back to school a little early after lunch, giving the soccer game a wide berth. The girls were in early as usual. They looked at me but didn't say anything. At twelve forty the boys came in noisily, but all the noise turned to silence when they saw me. Tad didn't meet my eyes.

Miss Stukey came in and told us to get out our reading books. She didn't look at me once but she knew I was there. Like Mr. Herndon, she had eyes in back of her head.

There was no recess that afternoon. The girls had gym, and we were supposed to work on the bulletin-board project. I worked alone, cutting out a design to go around it. Everyone kept away from me.

Finally school was over. I waited for Miss Stukey to call me up after class for an explanation, but she didn't. And I was grateful.

I walked out behind the others. They were shouting to each other.

"See you at practice, Tad."

"See you, Howard."

"Hey, Paul, you better quit clowning and get home if you're going to make practice on time."

"I will, man."

The guys on the team left the school as a group. I saw boys from other classes looking at them and then at me and I knew then that the whole school had heard about my running away this morning, and why I'd run away.

I walked home the long way. No more shortcuts.

Jane was home from junior high and was doing three things at once as usual: eating cookies, playing her radio, and doing her homework. When she saw me, she turned off the radio.

"Hello, Tim," she said, and from the way she said that, I knew she knew. Dad must have called her. "How are you?"

"OK," I said, and sat down on the couch.

"How was school?"

"OK."

"Isn't it a great day?"

"It's OK."

"Is that your big word for today?"

"Yes."

"Are you going to baseball practice now?"

"What business is it of yours?"

"None, but—"

"Then don't ask."

She turned on her radio. "I don't care whether you play baseball or not. Dad just called to ask me to remind you nicely that you had baseball practice. But obviously no one can talk to you nicely at all. Good-bye."

"Good-bye."

She turned the radio way up. I went out on the front porch. There were a lot of little kids out playing on the sidewalk, riding tricycles, chasing each other. One little kid was trying to hit a plastic ball with a plastic bat. He kept missing it and falling down. Another kid took it away from him to show him how and he missed and fell down too and they both laughed. Five years old looked a good age to be. No complications.

I went back into the living room and sat down. It was four thirty. Practice would be just starting. They'd play eight men on a side, except the team at bat would lend the team in the field a right fielder. They didn't need me. I'd just be the odd man. Dad didn't understand that. They had enough guys without me. But I'd promised him I'd go down. Well, I'd go down. They would have told Mr. Herndon all about it by now and he wouldn't want me to play. I'd just bike over and watch.

"I'm going," I called up the stairs to Jane.

"Where?"

"Over to the park."

"To practice?"

"Yes."

That wasn't a lie. That was where I was going.

"Try and be back by six."

"OK."

I got my bike out of the garage and rode over to the park. I could see them all on the diamond near the tennis courts. They were wearing their uniforms. That was another thing. I didn't have a uniform. Mr. Herndon wouldn't want me to play without a uniform.

I rode till I was about a hundred yards past the left fielder and in foul territory. Then I parked my bike and sat against a tree and watched them. None of them saw me.

They were in their practice game. Tad was pitching. He looked pretty good too, with great style on the mound. He struck out two guys while I watched.

It looked like the first team against the second. Tad, Howard, Ralph, Paul, Willie, Boomer, Charley Burns, Bobby Herndon, and Jeff Haynes against Scopus, Wilson, Glazko, Green, Tippit . . . and some other guys who didn't look like they knew what they were doing out there.

Tad was the first man up in his half of the inning and he hit the first pitch down the third baseline. The third baseman never had a chance, and the left fielder was slow getting started. The ball kept coming . . . right toward me.

Tad came around second and headed toward third. The left fielder finally got the ball and threw a pop fly to the shortstop. Tad had a triple. What's more . . . everyone had seen me sitting back here.

I got on my bike and started pedaling off.

I heard Mr. Herndon shout: "Foster! Tim Foster, come over here."

But I was far enough away to pretend I didn't hear. I kept pedaling, easily, as though I were taking a ride in the park.

"Foster," he shouted again.

Then I heard someone else shout, and it was a lot closer. I turned. Bobby Herndon was on a bike, coming after me.

He knew I'd seen him, so I stopped. Bobby came up to me.

"You left something at school," he said, and tossed me my glove. "And here's your ball."

He threw the ball at me. I had to get off the bike to get the ball. Bobby was chewing on a blade of grass, watching me. He was neither my friend nor my enemy. He was just the coach's son and a good ball player.

"My dad wants to talk to you."

"I don't want to talk to him."

"You want me to tell him that?"

"No."

"OK," he said, "let's go."

He wheeled his bike around and headed back to the ball diamond. I came after him.

"You're fifteen minutes late, Foster," Mr. Herndon said, as though that were the only thing that had gone wrong that day. "Get off your bike and warm up with Bobby. I'm going to put you in as soon as this inning is over. I want to see how you do in a game situation."

"You mean, I'm still on the team?"

"Keep coming late to practice and you won't be. Get a move on."

Obviously they hadn't told him what had happened.

Bobby Herndon got a catcher's glove and squatted down. I threw easily to loosen up my arm.

Every now and then I glanced over to see how Tad was doing as a pitcher. He threw a three-quarter overhand pitch, really an infielder's throw. It wasn't hard, but it was always around the plate and he seemed to be able to keep it low, forcing the batters to hit into the ground.

When the inning was over Mr. Herndon called out that I was pitching for Jeff Haynes' team. "Get in there, Tim. Jeff, you put on the catcher's gear."

I was pitching for the second team with Scopus, Wilson, Glazko, Randy Green, and the others. Although everyone got into the ball games in this league, none of the guys on this team ever started.

"All right, Tim," Mr. Herndon said, "I'll warm you up while Jeff is getting ready. You just throw them over the plate. No curves, no fancy stuff. Just rear back and throw them. Keep your eye on the target."

I threw a couple with some steam on them and Mr. Herndon nodded. "That will keep them on their toes. Batter up."

Jeff Haynes squatted behind the plate. Tad's team talked it up, while behind me my team was silent.

"Let's hear a little chatter out there," Mr. Herndon said. "Talk it up, infield."

There was a quiet murmur of nothing. I decided not to pay attention to either their silence or their chatter.

Boomer Gohane was up first. He waved the bat back and forth casually, his front foot extended slightly toward third, a pull hitter. I'd try to feed him outside pitches. If he got hold of an outside pitch, chances were he'd have to slice it into right field. I looked at my right fielder. He was playing deep, too deep, as though the guy at bat were a left-handed pull hitter.

"Come in a little," I called out to him.

He shouted back: "You play your game, Foster, and I'll play mine."

"Way to tell him off, Kevin," someone shouted from the team at bat. "But you'd better keep a close eye on your glove."

I winced. There was some laughter behind me.

"C'mon," Mr. Herndon called out, "let's get going."

I threw the ball at the outside corner. It was too wide. Boomer let it go for a ball.

"Way to look, Boom," the guys shouted.

"He's wild."

I kicked some dirt on the mound. My left foot had come down in the hole the other pitchers had made. I moved to the right a little bit. If I started on the rubber here I'd avoid the hole. A lot of pitching is in the feet, and if they aren't right, nothing else will be.

My second pitch was three feet over Boomer's head.

A chorus of cheers went up. Someone on my own team, behind me, laughed.

Jeff Haynes got another ball from Mr. Herndon and tossed it out to me. He hadn't said a word to me. He just squatted, made his target, and tossed the ball back.

I was determined to get the next pitch over. I aimed it right at Jeff's glove and took something off it. It bounced in the dirt a foot in front of Boomer.

"Let him walk you."

"He can't pitch."

"He can only do one thing well."

"Watch out for your gloves, guys."

Mr. Herndon called out to me: "Don't aim the ball, Tim.

Just throw it. Don't worry about walking him. This is a practice game. I want to see what your arm is like and your temperament too. And where's that chatter behind your pitcher, Scopus? You too, Randy. Talk it up. Let's hear a little chatter."

"Chatter, chatter, chatter," said Randy Green who was playing shortstop.

I walked Boomer on the next pitch. He tossed his batting helmet to Howard Kohn who was up next and trotted down to first. He and the first baseman laughed at something.

"Just relax and chuck away," Mr. Herndon called out.

Howard Kohn swung with a choked bat. I looked to see if my third baseman and first baseman were playing in. But they were both playing their normal positions.

"Watch out for the bunt, guys," I said.

"Why don't you get the ball over the plate first?" the first baseman said.

For a second anger welled inside me. I was tempted to heave the ball straight at him, but I forced myself to relax, holding my breath. This was part of their scheme to get back at me. Well, they had let me know. I would have to play my game and play it alone.

For some reason that decision relaxed me. I could count on no one but myself.

I checked the man at first and threw a strike at Howard Kohn. His bat didn't leave his shoulder. He swished it a couple of times, and settled back. I fired another one down the middle. He squared around and bunted it eight feet down the third base line. It was the third baseman's ball or the catcher's, but neither of them were moving. I went for it, picked it up, and held my throw. Howard was across first, and Boomer was on second.

I was about to say something to the third baseman when I realized he was grinning. So was everyone else in the infield, and on the sidelines, except for Mr. Herndon and he was frowning. He didn't say a thing. I guess he was thinking this thing had to work itself out naturally—even though this was more like war than baseball.

Tad was next up. Swinging two bats, he came up, threw one away, and dug in. With his baseball shoes and his wide open stance, he looked like a hitter all the way. All dug in for my fast balls. I decided to give him a big motion and threw a soft one.

It floated up there. Tad was out in front of it, and he missed, but Jeff Haynes, who had to be the world's worst catcher, missed the ball. Boomer took third and Howard Kohn took second.

I covered home, and when Jeff flipped the ball to me, I didn't say anything. They could play their game as much as they wanted to.

"Strike one," the umpire said. He was an adult recruited from the picnic benches.

My next pitch to Tad was a fast one down the middle. He got a piece of it and fouled it high in the air behind the plate. Haynes had room. I shouted that he had room, but he didn't move. He shook his head and asked Mr. Herndon for another ball. And the foul fell in front of the backstop, about fifteen feet behind him.

That was it. It was obvious what they were doing and they didn't care how obvious it was. And still Mr. Herndon said nothing.

"Nothing and 2," the ump called out.

Tad dug in. I decided to waste one and threw the next pitch outside. It was a little further out than I intended. Haynes made a weak stab at it, and it bounced off his mitt and went back to the backstop. I covered home. Boomer slid hard and I jumped. Howard Kohn was making a turn at third.

Jeff Haynes was picking up the ball nonchalantly, as if no one was on base. Howard was coming home too.

"Throw it," I begged Haynes.

He threw it all right—right in the dirt at my feet. It went through me. Howard scored standing up. No hits, two runs, no outs. One ball and two strikes on Tad Myers.

I walked back to the mound. The other team was shouting all kinds of things at me. My team was silent. Mr. Herndon leaned on one knee and watched. I wondered how long he'd let this go on. They were trying to force me off the team. Why didn't they all just walk off the field?

From then on Jeff Haynes didn't even bother to make a target for me.

I reared back and fired at the plate with everything I had. There was nothing to lose now. Tad took a big cut and missed it completely. Jeff Haynes, despite himself, held onto it.

Haynes didn't throw the ball around. He just tossed it at me.

"One out," the ump said.

Ralph Weyland was the next batter. The clean-up hitter, he stood deep in the box, but he was more of a plate crowder than Tad. I decided to throw it inside. He'd have a harder time coming around on it.

My first pitch sent him stepping back. He glared at me. "Try that again, Foster. Just try it again."

I sent the second pitch inside again. A fast one. Ralph stepped away, but this one caught the corner and the ump called it a strike.

Ralph protested, but the ump told him to get up there. On the next pitch, I gave Ralph the big motion and threw it soft. He was way out ahead of the ball.

"Strike two," the ump called.

I had him now, and I knew it. No one was on base; I could waste one. Let Jeff Haynes miss the ball. It wouldn't make any difference now.

I smoked one in there high and outside. Ralph waved at it. "Strike three," the ump said, and Haynes again for some odd reason held onto it. He threw the ball back at me.

My team said nothing. Good. Any encouragement from them would be phony.

I kicked the dirt around the mound, filling up a little hole I was making with my left foot.

Willie Warner was the next batter. He swung with a choked bat, a chop-type hitter.

To my surprise he bunted the first pitch, down the first base line. I hustled over, scooped it up and just as I was about to throw down to first base I was knocked sprawling onto the grass.

Willie rambled onto first.

I got up slowly.

"Baseline belongs to the runner," Willie said, grinning. "Remember?"

"All right, boys, that'll do it for today," Mr. Herndon called out.

"But we've only played two innings, Mr. Herndon," some-one said.

"Two innings of what?" Mr. Herndon snapped. "How not to support your pitcher? How to make errors behind him . . . on purpose? How guys on the same squad run into a teammate on purpose? That's not baseball. Bobby, get the equipment together. Kevin, give him a hand. You too, Warner. You're pretty good at knocking people down; let's see how good you are at picking them up. What's the matter with you guys anyway?"

Ralph Weyland spoke up. "The fact is, Mr. Herndon, we don't want Tim Foster on our team. He stole Tad Myers' glove. Maybe you don't know about that—"

"I know about it, all right," Mr. Herndon said grimly. His face was like granite. The words bit themselves off, and Ralph instinctively took a step backwards. "I know Foster found a glove in the park, and when he met the boy whose name was on the glove, I happen to know how hard he tried to get the glove back to that boy. I know he did wrong, and I know he also tried to do right. But I know someone else who did wrong without trying to do right."

"Who's that?" Ralph asked.

"You! You knew Foster was trying to get that glove back quietly to Tad, but you didn't let him. You had it all figured out, didn't you? You took the glove out of the bag, and let the cat out of the bag at the same time. Right?"

"OK, so I did. But I wanted to make sure Tad knew who had taken his glove."

"And now Tad knows. So does everybody else."

"But he took it, didn't he?"

"Yes, he did. But does that condemn him for life?"

"We don't want kids who steal things on our team, Mr. Herndon."

"Even when they've admitted they've made a mistake and are sorry?"

"He's not sorry, are you, Foster?"

It was a shrewd move. Ralph knew I couldn't say I was sorry to him. I could say I was sorry only to one person—Tad Myers. But Tad wasn't even looking at me. Tad was finished with me, and the others—they didn't want me on the team.

"Are you sorry, Foster?" Ralph repeated, sneering.

"I won't say I'm sorry to you, Weyland," I said.

I turned to Tad. For a second our eyes met.

"I'm sorry," I said to him.

He looked away, embarrassed. He didn't answer.

Willie Warner said: "This is disgusting. Does he really have to be on our team, Mr. Herndon? He's going to ruin the team."

"Nobody has to be on any team, Willie," Mr. Herndon said. "But so far I've seen no reason not to have a kid like Tim Foster on ours. He made a mistake, but he's apologized for it. Today, he came too late to practice, but I have a hunch he wasn't coming to practice in the first place. He just couldn't stay away. I think Foster has the arm and the temperament to be a first-class starting pitcher. We can go all the way with him and most of you know this. Also, he hustles. He hustled on the bunt the third baseman should have had, as well as on his own bunt. He covered home when Jeff Haynes was playing girl scout letting balls go through. Foster has convinced me that he's a battler. He didn't give up when he realized every man on his team was determined to make him look bad. He fought back by throwing hard and well.

"We're giving Tim Foster a chance to play for us because this game of baseball is known as the national pastime. It's supposed to stand for things like fair play and everyone having a chance. Foster is on this team because he has shown a great desire to play baseball and that's what this league is all about. And if those aren't enough reasons, let me add a final one: Tim's on this team because I, the coach of this team, say he's on. Now . . . any questions?"

"Yes," Ralph said, "how do I get off this team?"

"Just tell me you want out and I'll phone your name to the league president tonight."

"I want out."

"So do I," Howard Kohn said.

"Me too," Willie Warner said.

Jeff Haynes nodded. "I want off."

No one else spoke. Mr. Herndon looked around him. "Paul Nisbet?"

Paul grinned. "My uniform fits," he said.

"Bobby?" Mr. Herndon asked his own son.

Bobby gave a slow grin. "I guess I'll stick with my dad."

A laugh went up. But Mr. Herndon didn't smile. So far the count was 4–2 in favor of those leaving the team.

"Boomer?"

"I'll stick," Boomer said. "He didn't take my glove and I don't want to bat against him."

Another laugh went up. The count was now four going three staying.

"Kevin?"

"I'll do what Tad does."

"Charley?"

Charley Burns was the first-string catcher, a heavy-set quiet boy.

He nodded. "I'll do what Tad does."

"All right, Tad," Mr. Herndon said. "It looks like whether this team stays together rests with you. What about you?"

We all looked at Tad Myers.

»8«

To Quit or Not to Quit

"I don't want to play on the same team with Tim Foster," Tad Myers said quietly but firmly.

My heart sank. I'd hoped that maybe . . . but, I deserved it. I looked away.

"All right," Mr. Herndon said, "there's just one thing I can try to do and that's make a trade with another coach. We can't start the season with only nine players as well as some of you going away to camp or on vacation. I'll try to make a trade and I'll let you all know this evening."

"What about tomorrow's game against Mario's?" Boomer asked. "Is that still on?"

"Yes, it is. I want those of you who are staying on the team to be at the High School Field #2 at nine thirty tomorrow morning. Tim, I'll have a uniform for you this evening. I'll drop it over at your house."

"Do you want us there tomorrow, Mr. Herndon?" Ralph Weyland asked.

Mr. Herndon looked grim. "The only thing I want from you boys are your uniforms. You can bring them to my house tomorrow afternoon or night."

"When will we know what team we'll be on?"

"I don't know. I may have to make separate trades for all of you." They hadn't thought it out that far. They saw themselves going as a bunch to another team.

Ralph frowned. "If you can't trade us," Ralph said, "there'll be no Plumber team."

"That's probably right. But I'll do my best to trade you. See you in the morning." Mr. Herndon left and Bobby went with him, carrying the equipment bag. The rest of us stood there and no one knew what to say. They looked at me. I knew they were thinking I was the one to blame for the breakup of the ball club, and I guess I was.

Finally Ralph, who was always the spokesman in things like this, said: "There's only one person who can save the Warren Plumbers, Foster."

"Who's that?"

"You."

"How can I save the team?"

"By quitting it."

"It's a lot easier to trade one man than seven or eight," Howard Kohn said. "Unless you get off the team, there won't be any Warren Plumbers this season. And how will you feel about that?"

"C'mon, Foster," Ralph said. "Do one decent thing in your life. Before you moved into town we had a team. You came and now we've got no team. Take off, will you?"

Boomer Gohane spat out a weed. "Aw, leave him alone, Ralph. If you feel so bad about the team busting up, don't quit."

"Are you sticking up for him? A guy who steals gloves? How do you know he won't steal your bat?"

Boomer grinned. "I don't have a bat to steal. And I've seen yours—it isn't worth stealing. Hey, Foster, don't bother about Weyland's bat. There's not a hit left in it."

Even though Boomer meant well, I winced at his words. Why couldn't they let the incident with the glove be forgotten? How could I erase it from their memory? Not until I was able to erase it from my own, I suppose. And it would have to be by action, not words.

"C'mon, Boom," Paul Nisbet said, "let's go. See you, Foster."

"See you, Paul. See you, Boomer."

Paul and Boomer left. They had both been friendly toward me. Of those who remained, almost all were unfriendly. It was time for me to go before any more trouble started. I walked to my bicycle, but Ralph stepped in front of me, barring my way.

"Think about it, Foster."

"Think about what?"

"About quitting the team so we can have our team back the way it used to be before you showed up around here."

Anger burned through me, but I forced myself to relax.

"I won't quit, Ralph," I said quietly. "Not for you anyway. Now would you please step out of my way? I want to go home."

He didn't budge.

"Who would you quit for, Foster?"

I didn't answer him and moved to my right. He moved with me, still blocking my way. I wasn't afraid of Ralph; we were both the same size. And I wasn't really mad at him, nor at any of them. I knew how they felt about me.

"If Tad asked you," Ralph asked slyly, "you'd quit, wouldn't you?"

I hesitated.

"Wouldn't you quit if Tad asked you?"

"Yes," I said, brushing past him. Mounting my bicycle I pedaled away as fast as I could. Just before I cut around the hill I looked back to see if they were still there. They were, talking among themselves. I wondered if they were trying to get Tad to ask me to quit. I had said I would; I owed Tad Myers that much. But maybe they weren't asking him, and even if they did, maybe he wouldn't ask me. He was a decent guy. What a mess it was—and I had started it. But Ralph was helping it, and enjoying it.

My father and Jane were in the kitchen talking.

"Is that you, Tim?" my father asked.

"Yes."

"Come on in here a minute. How's your glove doing?"

"Pretty good."

It was his way of asking me how practice had been.

"I hear you've got a practice game tomorrow."

"How did you know?"

"Your coach and I had a talk today."

"Mr. Herndon?"

"Yes," my father said, grinning. "I gave him a call. I remembered what you said about his needing help, so I offered it."

That was how Mr. Herndon had found out about the glove. A lot of things became clearer.

"Are you going to help coach?"

"Starting tomorrow," my father said, "if you look down the third base line you may see a familiar figure there."

Jane laughed, and so did I. It had been a long time since my father had made light happy talk like that.

"Now if you two men will get out of my kitchen," Jane said, "I'll be able to get moving with supper."

"We can take a hint. Come on, Tim, let's throw a ball outside. If I'm going to coach, I'd better get in shape."

He hadn't offered to throw a ball with me since Mom died.

"Do you have your glove?"

"Right here. I dug it out of a trunk."

It was a wrinkled battered glove, smaller than mine. When I was very young, Mom, Jane, and I went to a night baseball game that Dad was playing in and at the time it had seemed very large. It looked small now.

"Don't look so worried about it," my father said, with a laugh, "it can catch anything you can throw. But do me a favor and lob a few first."

We played catch outside in front. I threw it easily and he threw it easily back at me and then each of us put a little more steam on it. Dad threw a "heavy" ball which zinged into my glove and I was glad I had padding. Anyone passing by could tell he was an old ball player, the way he caught it and tossed it back in one easy motion.

"When you were a kid, did they have Little Leagues?"

"No, we didn't have much organized ball until you got good enough to play Legion ball."

"How did you organize teams then?"

"We chose sides and played."

"Did you have uniforms?"

He laughed. "No."

"Who coached you?"

"Somebody's older brother. But mostly we played without coaching. We played baseball the way you ride bikes or go fishing. It was something every kid just did. Some were better than others, but some kids could catch more fish than others. There was always a vacant lot, or an empty field, and we plunked down and played. Nowadays with all the developments and houses, you have to reserve a field. I don't think you get in the baseball time we got in."

"How long would you play?"

"Oh, boy. Well, I can remember playing from nine in the morning to nine at night, and then as it got dark, we'd hit fungoes to each other, high in the air so you could see the ball against the sunset."

"I wish I'd been a kid when you were a kid."

"It's better now, Tim. You play better baseball than we did and you're learning more. You've got a fine team, and you can learn from just about everyone on your team. I like the way Mr. Herndon sounds over the phone. Low pressure. You're going to have a lot of competition behind you by the time you're seventeen, and you don't want someone pushing you too hard now."

Dad threw one low; I scooped it up.

"Nice catch, Tim."

I tossed it back and wondered if I ought to tell him what had happened today. He was going to coach tomorrow and had heard of Tad Myers and the others. They wouldn't be there. He'd either find out cold tomorrow, or I could prepare him by telling him now.

"Dad, I think I ought to tell you something about the team."

"Shoot."

"There isn't going to be much of a team out there tomorrow. Except for Boomer Gohane and Paul Nisbet, the best guys have quit."

"Why?"

"Because of me."

I told him what had happened that afternoon. He listened and didn't say anything. All the time we kept throwing the ball back and forth. It was a rhythm we had now; it was something tying us together that would never come untied.

Finally I told him how they'd asked me to quit and how I'd said I would if Tad asked me.

My father looked grave. "Do you mean you'll quit the team if Tad Myers asks you to quit?"

"He won't ask me."

"That wasn't my question."

"Yes . . . I'll quit. Besides I don't want to break up that team."

It was my turn to throw one in the dirt. Dad backhanded it easily and tossed it back underhand to me.

"Seems to me, Tim," he said softly, "that that team broke itself up. A team that doesn't fight to stay together isn't a team. Maybe you did Mr. Herndon a favor."

I shook my head. "You wouldn't say that if you could have seen his face. Tad Myers is the best all-around player in the League. He pitches, he plays shortstop, he bats third and clean-up."

"I don't care if he's a combination Bob Gibson, Rico Petre-celli, and Frank Robinson. You don't quit a team because you don't want to play with someone. I hope for his own sake Tad doesn't ask you to quit."

"I'll keep my fingers crossed. In fact, I've got them crossed right now."

"Why?"

"Because here comes Tad, Ralph Weyland, and Howard Kohn."

The three boys were coming down the street toward us. Dad glanced at them and then he said to me:

"Tim, you made one mistake, but after that you tried to do the right thing. Quitting now would be a mistake. Don't let them talk you into it."

"I gave them my word, Dad, but maybe they're not coming here anyway."

They stopped alongside us.

"Hi," I said, "this is my father. Dad, this is Tad Myers, Ralph Weyland, and Howard Kohn."

I took a chance; I was feeling desperate. "My father's agreed to help Mr. Herndon coach. Dad used to play semi-pro baseball."

My father knew what I was doing. He looked at the boys, and they looked away, avoiding his eyes in embarrassment. They couldn't very well ask me to quit a team my father was now helping coach. It had been a stroke of genius.

"Tim," my father said, "I'm going in and see how Jane's doing. Nice to meet you boys. Hope to see you out on the diamond."

"Nice to meet you," they managed to say, reluctantly.

No one said anything until my father was inside the house. Then Howard said: "Is your father really going to help coach?"

"Yes."

"Does Mr. Herndon know about it?"

"Sure. They talked this afternoon. My father used to earn a living partly by playing ball. He's an old shortstop."

Ralph and Howard looked at each other. Tad just looked uncomfortable, as though they'd made him come here— forced him to ask me to quit.

"I don't care," Ralph said to Howard. "It doesn't make any difference."

"I don't know," Howard said. He looked less sure.

"Look, what don't you know? It's either him or all of us. We agreed, didn't we? Go ahead, Tad."

Tad shook his head. "It's no good, guys."

"Do you want to play ball this summer with us?"

"Yes, but this is no good. Tim's father—"

"I don't care. We agreed. It's either him or us. And there's only one of him and nine of us."

They talked among themselves as though I were not standing with them. It was a measure, I thought, of how upset they were. Everyone had gone too far and no one would back up now.

Ralph turned to me. "You said you'd quit if Tad asked you to quit. Well, that's why we're here. We're sorry about your dad, but we've played for the Warren Plumbers for three years. We were a team long before you moved into town and we want to keep our team together. Go ahead, Tad, ask him."

Tad shook his head.

"C'mon, Tad, you promised. You can't let us down."

I felt sorry for Tad. I felt sorry for all of us, because we didn't have the courage to back down.

Tad said, without looking up, without looking at me, his face red: "Tim, would you quit so we could play on the Plumbers again?"

And now it was my turn for courage, but I failed as miserably as Tad had. "OK," I heard myself say, "I'll quit."

The moment I said it I felt all shaky inside. "I've got to go," I said, and ran in the house. I didn't look around. There was nothing to look back for, or forward to.

»9«

Mr. Herndon Has His Say

My father's head bowed.

"Bless O Lord this food to our use and us to Thy service."

"If your meat is overcooked," Jane said, "it's because you stayed out there so long with your friends."

"They're not my friends," I said.

"If they're not your friends, I don't know who they are. One of them was that boy you introduced to me. Tad Myers."

"Do you want to tell me what happened, Tim?" my father asked.

"Tad asked me to quit. He didn't want to, but they got him to."

"What did you say?"

"I said 'OK.' If they don't want me on their team, Dad, I

don't want to be on it. I don't even like baseball that much. There are lots of other things I'd rather do. I'd rather go fishing this summer, and you don't need eight guys to go fishing with. I want to go on bike hikes and see the country. I never liked baseball. I hated those games with everyone yelling at you—do this, do that, throw it to second, throw it home, and parents screaming at you all the time. It wasn't that way when you were a kid. You told me so yourself. And that's why you liked it. I hate baseball. I hate it around here. Why can't we go back home, Dad?"

I felt the tears coming, but I fought them down. I sat there and stared at my untouched plate.

My father said: "Tim, would you like to be excused from the table?"

I nodded.

"All right, you're excused. Go upstairs to your room and lie down. Jane, I'll finish Tim's plate. It's delicious . . ."

I went upstairs and lay down on my bed. The murmur of voices probably meant they were talking about me, but I didn't care.

After a while the dishes began rattling and I heard the screen door open and close, then the metallic rattle of the garbage can lid. You could close your eyes and follow everything happening in the house.

I wasn't mad or hurt any longer. I was tired and getting hungry. But I couldn't go down and ask for something to eat; I'd just have to change into my pajamas and go to bed. Should I call Mr. Herndon to tell him? He ought to be informed that I wouldn't play in tomorrow's game against Mario's, and the others would. But they'd probably tell him. Tad, Ralph, Howard . . . they had probably made a beeline to his house and were telling him everything was OK. The Warren Plumbers were back in business, and Tim Foster had quit.

"Tim," Jane said softly, outside my door.

"What is it?"

"I want to talk to you."

"What about?"

"Something private."

"I don't feel like talking."

"Then all you have to do is listen. It's important, Tim."

"Come on in."

She opened the door and stood there, taking it all in. Me lying in bed with my clothes on. She's got that big sister disgusted look. "Are you always going to be a baby and run away from the table?"

"It so happens I was excused by Dad."

"He excused you so you wouldn't make more of a fool of yourself than you were already doing."

"Is this what's so important to talk about?"

"No. I want to talk about your quitting the baseball team."

"If it's all the same to you, I'd rather not talk about it. It's my business."

"It's my business too, little brother."

"How did it become your business?"

"It became my business because we share the same father, and I'm worried about him."

"What's Dad got to do with it?"

"For the first time since Mother died, Daddy's beginning to act like his old self, getting out his glove and playing catch with you and offering to help coach your team. He's coming out of it now, Tim. And what do you do? Leave your team. What do you think that will mean for him?"

I was stunned. I hadn't thought of that. Even though I'd used my father to try and stay on the team, I hadn't thought of what my leaving would mean for him.

"Do you think he'll still want to coach your team if you're not on it?"

"No, I guess not."

"Tim, it's about time you started thinking about someone else beside yourself. This is a new town for all of us, a new job for Daddy, a new start in life. Just like that new baseball glove of yours, we all need a little breaking in. It's going to take time. But we can help each other. You can help Dad. I want you to go down there now and tell him you've changed your mind. You're not quitting the team."

"But I've quit already. I told those guys."

"You can call them up and tell them differently."

"Jane, I can't."

"You mean, you won't?"

"I mean I can't. I can't quit one second and then call them back and tell them I've changed my mind."

"For Dad's sake?"

"He wouldn't like that either."

"He wants you to play baseball, Tim. You know that."

"I can play next year."

"Can you?" she said with contempt. "I'll tell you what I think of you, Tim Foster. I think you're a coward."

Twenty-four hours ago I'd have jumped up and hit her, but I'd learned a lot since yesterday. Besides, I knew she was partly right—I didn't have the courage to lose face.

I just sat there.

"Shame on you, Tim Foster," Jane said, angrily. "You're a real baby."

She slammed the door behind her. A moment later I heard my father's heavy tread on the steps. He opened my door.

"Now what was that all about?"

"She's mad at me."

My father sat down wearily. "Why?"

I couldn't look him in the eye. "Because she says you want me to play ball and you'd help coach if I were playing ball and it was good for you to be playing ball with me again. You haven't done it since Mom . . ."

I couldn't go on.

My father was silent. "Jane said that," he said with wonder in his voice.

"Yes."

He shook his head. "I don't like seeing children grow up that fast." He looked at me. "There are lots of other things we can do together besides play baseball."

"But you love baseball."

"That's true. But it doesn't mean my son has to love baseball. There are lots of places a father and son can be together besides on a ball diamond."

"You mean, you don't mind my quitting?"

"I didn't say that. To be honest, Tim, I'm sorry you quit. You let those boys push you around. I don't think they're worth it. If Tad Myers is worth what you seem to think he is, he never would have come over and asked you to quit."

"They made him do it."

"He let them make him do it, and now you're letting them push you around too."

I hadn't thought of it that way.

Downstairs the front doorbell sounded. My father stood up. "It's been a long hectic day for you, Tim; I think you ought to get to bed early."

"Not now though."

"No," he smiled, "not now. I'll get it, Jane."

I sat there and listened to my father go down the stairs. I was lucky to have him as a father. He was a ball player and he didn't care whether I played ball or not. But I really wanted to play baseball: I loved it as much as he did. I wanted to be good too.

"Tim, would you come down here a moment?"

"Sure, Dad."

Mr. Herndon was in the living room talking with my father. I knew this was the first time they'd met face to face, but they were talking as if they were old friends.

"Hello, Tim," Mr. Herndon said, "I've brought your uniform along. How do you like it?"

He held up a baseball shirt that had WARREN PLUMB-ERS on the back. He tossed it to me, then pants, blue socks, and a blue cap with a big W on it.

"Try the pants and shirt on," Mr. Herndon said.

"We'd better hold up on this, Doug," my father said. "Tim, do you want to tell Mr. Herndon, or do you want me to tell him?"

"Tell him what?" I asked.

My father laughed. "What I wouldn't give to be young again and have total forgetfulness. I mean, tell him about your decision, about these boys coming over here."

"Oh." It was incredible, but I'd forgotten. Looking at the new uniform had made me forget.

"What's this all about, Tim?" Mr. Herndon asked.

I took a deep breath and told him what had happened.

"I see," Mr. Herndon said. "So you're quitting the team."

"Yes, sir. It's the only way for the team to get back together again."

"Is it now?" Mr. Herndon looked grim. "I'm not so sure of that, Tim. You see I wouldn't take those boys back right now if each of them was a potential major leaguer. If I did, they'd be running the team, not me. You're allowed to quit in this league, but you need the league's permission and the individual coach's permission to join a team. And I'm not giving that permission to any of them."

"Have you traded them yet?"

"Not yet. I'm meeting with another coach tomorrow afternoon after the game. I hope to get rid of at least three of them. As for you, I want you to think real hard about this decision to quit. You can quit, but you can't climb aboard that easily. And if I lose you, Tim, I guess I lose your dad. That makes me doubly sorry because I need help in running the team. And I'll tell you one more thing—you've got a future as a pitcher. You've got a strong arm and the ability to learn. Pitching is more than throwing, as your dad can tell you. But I can't teach you if you quit. And if you do, it just means that I can only field eight players tomorrow, not nine. Whether you're on my team or not, those other boys are off. Is that clear?"

"Yes, sir."

"What's your decision?"

I hesitated, for I didn't know what to say. My father was watching me.

"I'd like to stay on the Warren Plumbers, Mr. Herndon."

"Good, Tim. I was hoping you'd say that. Now go in another room and try on your uniform. The shirt may be a little big. It's supposed to last for two years. Bob," he said, to my father, "can you make tomorrow's game?"

"I sure can."

"I'd like you to coach third. As for signals . . ."

In the other room I tried on the uniform. The shirt was big but the pants fit well and the socks felt great. I looked at myself in the front hall mirror. WARREN PLUMBERS. I ran my fingers across the letters.

"Pull up your pants," my father said, coming in behind me.

Mr. Herndon laughed. "Can't have a starting pitcher with his pants falling down. Good night, Tim. Good night, Bob."

While Dad was seeing Mr. Herndon to the door, I pounded an imaginary ball into my glove, then wound up and sent it flying to home plate.

"Strike one," Jane said.

I blushed, but she wasn't laughing at me. She was smiling and kind of proud too.

"If I can only pitch a good game tomorrow. Suppose I get knocked out of the box."

"Then," my father said, coming back in, "you'll join a long list of pitchers that includes Bob Gibson, Sandy Koufax, Lefty Grove, Walter Johnson, Christy Mathewson . . ."

"Gee," Jane said, "I thought Tim might be good, but not that good."

"He isn't," Dad said. "All those pitchers always did one thing the night before a big game that Tim hasn't done yet."

"What's that?" I asked.

"They ate supper."

We all laughed.

"Hungry?" Dad asked.

"Starving," I said.

"Good," old Jane said, "I've kept your supper warm in the oven."

"Lead me to it," I said.

I ate in my uniform. I would have slept in it too, but Dad said great pitchers always wore pajamas to bed.

»10«

Pitching for the Plumbers

They say the other team always looks bigger than yours. In this case it was true. Mario's Supermarket were big, looking like sixth or seventh graders. They all wore baseball shoes and warmed up along the third baseline with the confidence of a team that has won three straight league championships.

Some of them knew Boomer Gohane and said hello to him and to Paul Nisbet. But after a few curious glances at the rest of us, they proceeded to ignore us.

Mr. Herndon dumped open the ball bag.

"OK, loosen up, guys. Tim, throw with Paul Nisbet. He's going to be our catcher today. Bob?" Mr. Herndon looked questioningly at my father.

Dad grinned. "You may not want to use me, Doug, but I'll warm up."

Everyone laughed. The guys on the team were all pleased my father was helping out. And I could see them watching out of the corners of their eyes how my dad caught and threw. They could tell he was a pro from the way he snapped the ball off and zinged it into Mr. Herndon's glove.

"Your old man can throw, can't he?" Paul Nisbet said.

"And hit too," I said proudly. "He used to play in an industrial league back home."

"Boy, we could sure use him if he was a little younger," Tom Scopus said. Tom was playing first in place of Ralph Weyland. Even though he wasn't much of a ball player he had a sense of humor, and maybe humor would help us through the next few games.

"Throw easy, Tim," Paul said. "There's no one to relieve you. You've got to go all the way."

"Who're their big hitters?"

"You see that big red-headed guy there, throwing by the tree?"

"Yeah."

"That's Kearney Boylan. He's the best hitter in the league and also their pitcher. There won't be anything you can do about him. You've got to watch out for Casey Birdwell too. He's the catcher and he hits a long ball. The shortstop Marchessini, over there, talking with their coach, is a good ball player. They're all fast too, Tim. You've got to keep them close."

I grinned. "How does your arm feel, Paul?"

Paul giggled. "I caught once in the eight-year-old league and I threw it back to the pitcher on one bounce."

"Great."

"But I'll reach you on a fly today."

I laughed, took a few steps back and threw harder.

"Ouch," he said. "I'm not used to this position. You throw harder than Tad."

"Hey," Randy Green said, "speak of the devil. Look what's arrived?"

He pointed toward a small hill behind third base. Coming over the crest of it were six or seven kids on bicycles. Tad Myers, Ralph Weyland, Howard Kohn, Charley Burns, Willie Warner . . .

"Hello, quitters," Tom Scopus called out merrily.

The boys on Mario's Supermarket team looked up astonished at Tad and Ralph and the others.

"Aren't you guys playing ball anymore?"

"We fired the whole bunch of them," Scopus said.

"All right, fellas," Mr. Herndon said, "forget about the audience. We're here to play ball."

But it was hard not to notice the onlookers. They got off their bikes and sat on the grass behind Mario's bench. It was obvious whom they were rooting for.

"All right, Plumbers," Mr. Herndon called out, "let's have some infield and outfield. Tim, go on warming up with Paul. Bob, will you catch for me? Let's hustle out there, guys."

As soon as the team was set, Mr. Herndon began slapping ground balls around. The first one to Bobby took a bounce over his head.

"We'll try it again. And use your chest, Bobby. That's why God gave third basemen barrel chests."

Bobby gloved the next grounder and threw it over to first. Tom Scopus, who hadn't any arm at all, threw it home in the dirt. Dad backhanded it and whipped it back to third. Bobby caught it and yelled. "Ouch, Mr. Foster."

Mr. Herndon laughed. "That's how Paul's going to peg them down there when someone tries to steal."

"In your dreams, man," Paul said softly to me, as we threw the ball back and forth.

"What about signals?" I asked.

He grinned. "One for a fast ball, two for a curve, three for a slider, four for a change of pace, five for a knuckle ball and that's all the fingers I'm carrying today."

I laughed. "We'd better stick to two. One for a fast ball and two for a change of pace."

"Sounds good to me."

"Hey, Nisbet," Ralph Weyland called out, "you can't catch."

"Why don't you guys go chase girls?" Tom Scopus said.

Paul shook his head. "I'd like to win just to show those guys."

"Wag your fingers when you want me to throw to first."

"OK. Let's practice."

I threw according to Paul's signals. Even if it did nothing else, it slowed me up, gave me a rhythm. I knew that if things started going badly for me out there, I'd tend to pitch faster and faster. The signals would take care of that. They would also help Paul take charge of the game. The catcher, as my dad often explained to me, is the only guy who can see what everyone is doing. He's the one in charge.

We threw for about five minutes and then infield practice was over and the guys came trotting in. Dad came over and stood behind me.

"Keep following through, Tim," he said quietly. "You'll

throw a lot of high pitches unless you follow through."

I went over my signals with him and he thought it was OK. Then he walked over to the bench and I heard him talking to the infielders.

"Randy, Steve—on throws to second, who covers?"

"I do when it's a left-handed hitter," Randy said. "Otherwise it's Steve."

"That's right. Who's calling pop-ups?"

"Bobby."

"What happens when an outfielder and an infielder are after the same pop-up?"

"The one who hollers the loudest gets it."

"No. The outfielder can call off the infielder. It's easier to run forwards than backwards. Who's the cutoff man on balls to the right side . . ."

And so it went. I continued to throw with Paul. The tension was building in my stomach. I'd busted this team up, so I had to do well for them now.

A short sunburned man came over. This was the coach of Mario's—Mr. Marchessini, the father of the shortstop. Mr. Herndon introduced him to my father, and they shook hands.

"I hear you've had some troubles," Mr. Marchessini said.

"Bad news has swift legs," Mr. Herndon said. He glanced at Tad, Ralph, Howard, and the others lying in the grass behind Mario's bench.

Mr. Marchessini nodded in that direction. "If they start bad-mouthing anyone, out they go," he said grimly.

"Bad-mouthing us or you?" Mr. Herndon said, his eyes twinkling.

The three coaches laughed. They discussed ground rules,

and who would ump. Mr. Marchessini volunteered a spare father.

"It's either him or Bob Foster here. And it never did a kid any good to have his father breathing right behind him calling balls and strikes. Of course, after we knock your boy off the mound, you can come in and ump, Bob."

"Can't knock him out, Coach," my father said drily, "he's all we've got. And he'll do, anyway."

"Better tell your man to call them from behind the pitcher. We've got no one to call them on bases."

"I'll do that. Might as well get started. Nice to meet you, Bob."

"Same here."

They all shook hands and Mr. Marchessini left.

"I'm going to read the lineup now," Mr. Herndon said, "then Mr. Foster will go over batting signals. Art Tippit, first up and playing second. Paul, number two and catching. Bobby, number three and playing third. Boomer, take that milkweed out of your mouth."

"Yes, sir," Boomer said, taking it out with one hand, and unconsciously reaching for another with his other hand.

"Boomer Gohane, clean up and center field. Randy Green, shortstop and fifth. Tim Foster, pitching and batting sixth. Steve Glazko, left field and seventh. Tom Scopus will play errorless ball at first and bat eighth—"

"Yes, sir," Scopus said.

"Bill Wilson, batting ninth and playing right field. OK, guys, before I turn you over to Mr. Foster for instructions about signals, a couple of words. Mario's is ready to be taken. They're cocky and superior and they don't know it yet, but they're riding for a fall. We're the boys that can drop them

—if everyone gives it his all, plays errorless ball, thinks what he's doing. And gets some hits. Kearney isn't going to walk anyone. He never does. Let's swing that bat. OK, Bob."

Dad moved in front of the team. "We'll keep things simple," he said quietly. He wore an old baseball cap of his and he wore spikes. The guys liked that touch. He was a ball player and he looked it. "We'll only use two signals. Three with a wipe-out. Bunt signal is hands on hips. It might be the fifth move I make. Watch me. I might touch elbows, cap, side, hands on hips, peak of cap again. When you see hands on hips, the bunt's on. Take signal when the count's three and zero is touching my shoes, and that might come in any order. First thing I do, last thing I do. When I want to wipe out the bunt and take, I'll take my cap off. You can't miss that. OK?"

"What about stealing?"

"I like boys to steal on their own," my father said. "I like to see you running. If I think you ought to go down, though, and you're not making any bold moves, I'll rub my hands together. First base coach, whoever he is, keeps an eye on me. And if the runner misses it, he rubs his hand. Batter, look for that signal too. Protect that runner if he's going down. Square around for a bunt. If you can afford it, take a swinging strike. Any questions?"

"We won't steal much on old Casey, Mr. Foster," Randy said. "Watch his arm."

Kearney Boylan was just delivering the last of his warm-up pitches. Casey Birdwell threw the ball on a line to second. That ball didn't travel more than ten feet off the ground. My heart sank. Paul Nisbet shook his head. "Man, is he ever going to make me look bad."

"They know you're an outfielder, Nisbet," Steve Glazko said.

"They'll know it when Paul throws it into the outfield," Scopus said.

"Ha. Funny."

"All right, guys. Let's go. Tippit, get up there."

Dad trotted out to the third base coaching box. Bill Wilson went to coach at first.

"Talk it up," Mr. Herndon said.

"C'mon, Art. Start things off."

"He can't pitch, Art."

"A little bingle, Art."

"He throws meat balls. Pitcher throws meat balls."

It was wishful thinking, I decided. Kearney Boylan looked ten feet tall on the mound. He kicked the dirt a little this way and then a little that way, shaping up the mound to his own liking. He knew exactly where he wanted his left foot to come down. He knew a lot of things I didn't know yet; I'd learn by watching him.

Art Tippit stepped in. Kearney Boylan didn't go to a wind-up. He pitched from a stretch position with a nice easy relaxed motion. But there was nothing easy about the way the ball zinged in there.

Old Tippit must have thought so too because he just stood and blinked while two strikes were called on him.

"C'mon, Art," Mr. Herndon shouted. "Let's get that bat off your shoulders."

"Guard that plate, Art."

"Be tough in there, Art," my father called out. "Those balls are coming straight in."

Art was determined to swing on the third pitch. It was

outside but he swung and he caught the end of it and sent a dribbler down the first base line. The first baseman gobbled it up, stepped on the bag and they whipped it around their infield.

"That's OK, Art," Mr. Herndon said. "You got a piece of the ball. Next time wait till it's in the strike zone and you'll send it out of here. That fast ball's a good ball to hit. Remember this: the faster it comes in, the faster it goes out."

"You mean, the faster we go out," Tom Scopus said nervously.

"Talk it up, guys."

"C'mon, Paul. Get ahold of one."

Paul glanced down at my father who gave him a flurry of signals, including the bunt signal.

Kearney pitched. Paul came around. The pitch was high. The third baseman was charging in. Paul got his bat back.

"Ball one."

Once again Paul got a flurry of signals from my father. The third baseman watched them too. He must have decided the bunt was off, because he lay back. But the bunt was still on.

Kearney threw a high fast one. Paul gave a little chop swing and the ball bounced about ten feet down the line. It would be a close play, but Paul was fast. He flew down the line. The third baseman barehanded the ball and in one underhand motion whipped it across the diamond, but Paul's flying feet hit the bag an instant before the ball arrived.

"Safe," the ump shouted.

And you would have thought he'd hit a home run the way our bench talked it up.

"Well, that ties our record of last year," Scopus said. "We got a single off of Kearney last year too."

Paul put on a running helmet and Bobby stepped in.

"One away. Look alive, Paul."

Paul took a good lead off first. Kearney glanced around his left shoulder at him and stepped off the rubber. Paul went back. Kearney stepped on the rubber. I liked the way Kearney took his time. He was sizing up the situation. Paul's lead was too long but Kearney didn't feel he was ready to throw to first. He'd be ready now. He was. He whipped across a hard knee-high throw. Paul drove back head first. Safe, but not by much.

"Boy, what a motion he's got," I said.

Paul took his big lead again. And again Kearney threw, but this time the ball almost got away from their first baseman. Our bench was shouting.

"He'll throw it away, Paul."

"You've got him worried, Paul."

Another big lead. Kearney looked at him, leaned back and threw wide to the plate. A pitch out. Casey jumped up with the ball, his right arm cocked, but Paul ducked back into first.

"Way to go, Paul," Mr. Herndon shouted.

Kearney was ready again, but Bobby stepped out of the box. Already it was a war of nerves, and we were only in the top half of the first. I wondered what Tad and Ralph and those others were thinking. They were still there behind Mario's bench, not shouting, just watching. They probably thought we'd fold up without them. I think we were now surprising them, as well as Kearney Boylan.

I saw my father rub his hands together. Paul took his big lead. Kearney glanced around, then pitched to the plate. Paul took off. He had a good jump. Bobby squared around to fake a bunt. He drew his bat back. Casey Birdwell had the ball and fired it down to second. Paul slid. It was close, but he was out. A perfect throw had to beat him and a perfect throw it was.

The market team began shouting.

"Well," Scopus said, "his arm didn't get any worse over the winter."

"He was right on," Mr. Herndon said. "Good try, Paul. You almost had it. That was a smart play."

Paul was huffing and puffing. He sat down next to me. "Your dad sent me down. I'd never have tried it against Casey's arm, but I'm going to beat him the next time. I didn't even get a good jump and I almost made it."

He had got a great jump, I thought, but here he was, beat at second but not beaten, ready to come back. It was a good sign. The Warren Plumbers were very much alive.

Getting that second out seemed to add something to Boylan's arm. He reared back and threw two fast balls by Bobby Herndon and our side was out.

"OK, guys," Mr. Herndon said, "hustle out there. He can't throw that hard all day. We'll get to him. No mistakes. Concentrate out there. Tim, just get out there and chuck to Paul's mitt. Just fire them in there as if you are at Sampson Park. No temper, all relaxed. Paul, don't let him work too fast . . ."

I walked out to the pitcher's mound. Dad and I crossed paths. He had a tiny grin on his face. As we went by, he winked at me. "Go get'em, Foster," he said.

It was a funny moment. As though we were teammates, at last.

The ump brought me back to reality. "Six warm-ups, Tim," he said.

I stepped on the rubber and Paul Nisbet squatted down forty-five feet away. The butterflies which had disappeared while we were batting were now back, making a traffic jam in my stomach. I threw my first pitch six feet over Paul's head.

"That's his best pitch too," Ralph Weyland called out to the Mario's bench.

My other five pitches were wild too, but they seemed to be getting in the range.

"Coming down," Paul shouted, after my fifth pitch.

He threw it down to second on a bounce. The ball went through Art Tippit's legs, and Boomer came in and lobbed it back into Tippit.

A lot of jeers went up from Mario's, added to by Ralph and Willie Warner.

"He can't pitch and they can't play," Ralph said.

"He's a nothing pitcher from Nowheresville," Willie Warner said.

"Beat him for us, Mario's," Kevin Reilly said.

I felt a thrust of anger, but I tried to calm myself by kicking the dirt. Don't lose your temper, I said to myself. Don't blow it all.

Mr. Marchessini, Mario's coach, turned around and told our ex-teammates to shut up or get out. They shut up but they grinned and made all kinds of gestures. Not Tad. He just sat there, cross-legged, and watched. A little sad, I thought.

"Batter up," the ump said.

"Blow it by them, Tim," Paul Nisbet shouted. And out in center field old Boomer called to me:

"Picking cherries, Tim. Picking cherries."

I didn't know what he meant by that, but it sounded funny and I grinned.

Before the inning was over, my grin was gone.

»11«

First Inning Blues

My first pitch of the inning was my best one—it only went a foot over the batter's head.

"Hey, get a ladder."

"Where'd he come from?"

"Wild, wild. The pitcher's wild."

"Hey, Tad, is this the guy they traded you for?"

"Look out, Ritchie, for the next one you'll need an airplane."

"Don't listen to them, Tim," Paul called out.

"No batter in there," Steve Glazko said behind me.

"Talk it up, infield," Mr. Herndon called out.

I didn't feel loose. My muscles were tight and my stomach was still full of butterflies. The mound didn't feel comfort-

able like the mounds back home. There was a hole in front
of the rubber where other pitchers had stood. My right foot
sank into it. My left foot was coming down in the hole
Kearney Boylan had made for himself. I was pitching in
his spot, not in my own, and I didn't know what to do
about it.

"Here we go, Tim," Paul called out. "No stick up here."

He wiggled one finger at me. The batter, a tall thin kid
whose jaws worked over a piece of gum, waved his bat. I
don't know why bubble gum should make a kid look tough
at the plate, but it does.

Aim it lower, I thought. Aim at his knees.

Paul lowered his glove. I threw at it. It was a good pitch.
Straight as an arrow, and low. The kid's bat came around.
Crack! The ball took off like a shot. It went over Randy
Green's head at shortstop and was bouncing between the
left fielder and Boomer in center.

"All the way, Ritchie," Mario's bench was shouting.

"Run hard. You've got it made."

"Third," Randy Green shouted.

Boomer caught up with the ball, whirled, and fired it
toward third. It was a good low throw but it skidded in the
grass and went through Bobby Herndon's legs. No one was
backing him up. The one who should have been was me.
I was caught watching the play, just like a spectator. The
runner came around third and scored standing up.

"You're supposed to back up third on that play, Tim,"
was Mr. Herndon's comment. Just a couple of days ago I
would have got mad at that. He didn't say anything about
his son missing the ball at third, but I knew now he was try-

ing to teach us baseball. If someone missed a ball, he missed it. And he knew it. But a player didn't always know where he was supposed to be.

I glanced at my father. He sat on the bench, his cap pulled down against the sun, his hands clasped. Motionless. I wondered what he was thinking—waiting for me to blow up? I wasn't going to lose my temper, that much I knew.

A player from Mario's retrieved the ball. "Try backing up home on the next pitch," he called out to me.

"Hey, pitch," someone else called out, "your socks smell."

I kicked the dirt a little, trying to fill in Kearney Boylan's hole.

"Look at him kick the dirt. He's mad."

"Pitcher's got a temper."

"Pitcher's wild, wild, wild."

"Hey, Pitch, is it true you broke up the Plumbers?"

"The plumbing, man, not the Plumbers."

They started laughing.

I remember Dad telling me that riding a pitcher was part of the game and that if I ever wanted to be a good pitcher I'd have to lose my rabbit ears. If you teach yourself not to pay attention, after a while you don't hear.

Right now, though, I heard all right.

"These guys are all lip, Tom," Art Tippit called out from second base. "They hit with their mouths."

"No batter in there," Tom Scopus called out.

But the Mario team kept riding me, and I kept hearing them, so I decided one way to make them shut up would be to show them how hard I could really throw.

Paul gave me the one finger for a fast ball. I went to a full wind-up and threw it as hard as I could.

"Look out!"

The batter hit the dirt. The ball went flying over his head and hit against the backstop. It wasn't that close to him, but he made a drama out of it.

And the bench reacted: "Boy, isn't he a prize package?"

"You carry a knife, too, Pitch?"

"You'd better look out when you get up, Pitch. Kearney can throw twice as hard as that."

Paul Nisbet trotted out to the mound with the ball.

"Man," he said, with a little grin, "don't do that again. You make them mad and you half scared me to death."

"It slipped."

"I know that. But do *they* know that? Take it easy. Let them hit it. Our guys will get them out for you."

"You believe that?"

"I'll let you know soon as they hit one."

He was trying to relax me and I appreciated it. But it was hard to relax when faced with their bench's jeers, and with the ex-Plumbers sitting silently behind it, wishing me bad luck. There was also my father, watching me pitch for the first time, quiet but not missing a thing.

Paul signaled a slow pitch. I wound up and threw. It was way outside and rolled to the backstop.

"Look out below."

"You'd better get two catchers, Pitcher."

"Look out, Jack. The next pitch'll be behind you."

Mr. Herndon called time and trotted out to the mound. "You're trying too hard, Tim. You're fighting this game instead of pitching it. Just relax and let them hit it. That was a good pitch you threw to the first batter. He hit it well. No crime in that. Just keep letting them hit it. They'll start hitting them for outs, and you'll get yourself a rhythm and be all right. Remember, you're our only pitcher right now. There's no one warming up behind you." He patted me on the back.

Paul signaled the slow pitch again. I threw it up there just as though it was batting practice. A little outside. The batter reached across the plate and hit it into right field. An easy play if Paul Nisbet were playing his regular right field position, but Paul was catching, and Randy Green just stood there until it was too late. Then he charged in. The ball bounced in front of him. The runner made a wide turn. Randy had the sense to throw it to second.

"A little slow out there, Randy," Mr. Herndon shouted. "That's the way to chuck, Tim."

I looked over at first. Tom Scopus was holding the runner on. He wasn't a very good ball player and I knew I'd be taking a chance throwing over to first. Maybe I could bluff the runner back with a few hard looks.

Their number three batter was Tom Marchessini, Mario's shortstop. He knocked the dirt out of his spikes and stepped in, waving a big bat. He looked pretty good up there.

"He's no hitter, Tim," Paul yelled.

"Watch the runner, Pitch. He's going down," someone on their bench yelled.

I went to my stretch position and glanced at first. The runner was taking a big lead.

"C'mon, Pitch," he called out to me, "throw it."

I whirled and threw it. We had him leaning the wrong way, but Tom took his eyes off the ball. It bounced off his glove, and the runner went on to second standing up.

"Sorry, Tim," Scopus said sheepishly.

"That's OK, Tom," I said. "We'll get another crack at that guy."

I didn't feel like saying that. I felt like kicking him in the rear end.

"Good move anyway, Tim," Mr. Herndon called out.

The move quieted Mario's bench a little, but not much.

"Look out, Pitch. He's going to steal third."

"Forget about him, Tim," Paul called out, "Bobby and I can handle him. Work on the batter."

Stepping on the rubber, I looked back to second. The runner was taking an enormous lead. Art Tippit was making no attempt to keep him close. I stepped off the rubber. The runner darted back.

"Balk, balk," yelled the Mario's bunch.

"No balk," the ump said. "He doesn't have to follow through on throws to second."

"Keep him close, Art," I called out.

Art moved over toward second. I threw to the plate. An off-speed pitch which Paul had signaled for. Marchessini timed it perfectly, waiting on it till the last second. Crack. My heart sank. The ball went sailing over our left fielder's head—an easy home run. I ran to back up the plate, but there was no play. Marchessini trotted across the plate, home by the time our left fielder was throwing the ball back. Three to nothing and still no one out.

Paul walked back to the mound with me. "That's OK, Tim," he said.

"It's just great," I said.

He grinned. "Maybe we'd better go back to fast ones."

"OK."

"We'll get those runs back. I promise you."

"I'm all right, Paul. I'll get the fast one in."

I did just that. Kearney Boylan was the next batter. He had a wide open stance and looked like a fast ball hitter, but I figured our only hope was for me to throw hard. Kearney at least offered a big strike zone.

I burned it in there and Kearney, first pitch swinging, belted the ball on a line into right field at Bill Wilson. As with a lot of inexperienced outfielders, Bill instinctively came in when he should have been working out. Too late he realized his mistake and turned, but the ball was over his head.

"All the way, Kearney."

"Stand up, Kearn. Stand up."

"Nice chuck, Pitch."

"Where did they ever find that guy?"

Four-nothing and no outs. I looked over at Mr. Herndon and my dad, but neither of them said anything. For better or for worse (and it looked like it was for worse) I was the pitcher.

The number five man in their batting order was their big catcher Casey Birdwell.

"Wait on the gopher ball, Case," their bench called out.

Paul called for the fast one. I threw it. To my surprise, to Paul's surprise, and to Bobby Herndon's surprise at third base, Casey bunted. Four runs ahead and he bunts! It caught us all flatfooted. Bobby had to let it roll, hoping it would roll foul. But it stayed fair. We stared at the ball.

"Wake up!" Mr. Herndon shouted, "he's going for two."

Casey, taking advantage of the general confusion, had rounded first and was heading for second. Bobby pounced on the ball and threw it hurriedly toward second. It bounced in the dirt in front of Art Tippit. He couldn't hold onto it and Casey was in with a bunt double. Mario's team was laughing.

"We could have had him, Bobby, if you'd have got that throw up," Art Tippit said angrily.

"Go stuff it," Bobby muttered.

"Come on, infield," Boomer called out, "play baseball."

"You guys aren't doing so well out there either," Tom Scopus retorted.

"Hey," I said, "let's play together. They're giving us a bad enough time without us making it worse."

"Now look who's talking?" Tippit said. "Let's face it, Foster, you're giving them nothing but fat pitches."

"Here comes Mr. Herndon," Steve Glazko said. "Maybe he'll put Bobby in. Even Bobby can pitch better than Foster."

I took a deep breath and said nothing. They were bitter and I was the logical one for them to be bitter about. Mr. Herndon was stomping toward us from the bench. When he came out to the mound, I was finished pitching, for it would be his second mound visit in one inning.

To my surprise, he paused on the foul line and cupped his hands.

"Ump, I want to have a meeting of my whole team if it's OK with you. This is not a visit to the pitcher."

"OK with me," the ump said, "but make it fast."

"I will," Mr. Herndon said, biting off his words. "All right, all of you in here. On the double."

Everyone came round. A team meeting in the middle of a game—I could not remember such a thing ever happening.

For a second Mr. Herndon said nothing. His eyes, cold and angry, lingered on each man. When he spoke, he spoke tersely. "Slop," he said. "This is pure slop. A few hits and you start picking on each other. A bunch of ninnies. That's all you are. And you call yourself a ball club. A ball club helps each other out when things are going badly. A ball club talks it up when things are bad. You're quitters, each one of you. Blaming the next guy. Well, you're going to stay out here if the score is one hundred to nothing. And it will be unless you get behind your pitcher. Talk it up for him. Ride the other team, not your own. Now let's play baseball. That's what we came here to do."

Mr. Herndon turned abruptly and left. We stood there a moment and then we broke up and went back to our positions. There was silence behind me, broken by Steve Glazko just as I put my foot on the rubber.

"No batter, Tim. No batter in there, big Tim."

I threw my fast ball. The batter squared around to bunt. Bobby and Tom Scopus came running in. The batter got his bat back in time. It was high. Ball one.

"Way to chuck, Tim," Bobby said. "He's a looker in there."

I threw the next pitch in the same place, high. The batter swung and hit it on a line over shortstop for a single. Bill Wilson, playing too far in, caught it on one bounce and Casey, rounding third, decided to come back to third. It was a good play by Bill Wilson.

"OK, they got a lucky hit. That's the way to play, Wilson," Mr. Herndon called out.

I knew the runner on first would be going down, since

Casey was on third. He did on the very next pitch. Paul feinted throwing to second and cocked to throw to third, but Casey was standing on the bag, grinning from ear to ear. One catcher rarely fooled another.

"That's OK, Tim," Tom Scopus called out. "We're closing the gates on these big bums."

I got the next pitch in and the batter popped it up. An easy out.

"I got it," Art Tippit said.

"I got it," Steve Glazko said.

They both stepped aside at the last second and the ball fell safely between them. Casey scored and the runner on second moved on to third.

Tippit and Glazko glared at each other and for a moment I thought it was going to start all over again, but then Art said: "My fault, Steve."

"No," Steve said, "I heard you shout."

"Heck," Bobby Herndon said, "I'm the one supposed to be calling infield pops. It was my fault."

A comical error, but we hadn't fallen apart. In fact, we were coming together at last. I knew from that moment on things were going to get better. Certainly they couldn't get any worse. One thing was better already: my butterflies were gone. And I wasn't pushing the ball, aiming it . . . I was throwing it up there and they were in the strike zone. Mario's were good hitters, but sooner or later our guys would start catching the ball.

I would like to report that it was sooner rather than later, but it would not be the truth. Before that inning was over, Mario's scored nine runs. They hit me from one end of the park to the other. Finally Tom Scopus caught a pop-up, and Paul Nisbet caught a pop foul, and a great sarcastic cheer went up from Mario's side of the field.

We walked slowly off the field, feeling as if we'd been out there all day.

Dad's path and mine crossed. "You threw a lot of pitches, Tim," he said, "but you've got a rhythm now, haven't you?"

"Yes."

"It will be a new ball game from now on. You'll see."

"Gohane up. Green on deck. Foster in the hole. OK," Mr. Herndon said, "they got nine runs. We can get nine runs. Don't try to murder the ball. Just meet it up there. Let's go, Boomer."

Boomer Gohane stepped up to the plate.

"Give it a ride, Boom."

"Big hole in left center, Boomer."

"Hey, Boylan, your socks smell."

"Let's go, Plumbers."

It was amazing. You would have thought it was the bottom of the ninth and the score tied. We weren't acting at all like a team that was nine runs behind. We were going to win this game.

»12«

Plumbers Fight Back

Kearney Boylan reared back and shot his fast ball over the plate. Boomer swung and the crack of the bat brought us to our feet. The ball shot over the shortstop's head and into left field. Boomer made a wide turn at first and came back to the bag.

For a moment we were silent, and then it broke loose. We were all shouting. I even heard a couple of our ex-team-mates call out. Tad said: "Good hit, Boomer."

And Ralph Weyland added: "Way to go, Boom."

Paul laughed softly. "Once a Plumber always a Plumber."

"OK, Randy," Mr. Herndon said, "let's have a little hit. We need base runners."

I thought he was telling Randy not to try to bunt his way on. It's always tempting to try to bunt against a pitcher you don't think you can get your bat around on. But Kearney threw high fast balls, the hardest kind to bunt. We didn't need any sacrifices either. We needed base runners and runs.

Randy was neither to bunt nor swing. He just stood there and watched three fast balls whizz by him for strikes. Some of the heart went out of our chatter.

I took the doughnut off my bat and stepped in there.

"Left center's wide open, Tim," Dad called out from his coaching box.

"Pitchers can't hit, Kearney," their first baseman said.

I decided to choke up a little. Just meet the ball, I told myself.

Kearney sidearmed me on the first pitch. I stepped away and the ball whipped by me.

"Strike," the ump said.

"Oh, no," I said.

"Oh, yes," Casey Birdwell sang out, and everyone laughed.

"Stick in there, Tim," Dad called out.

I had bailed out but I was determined not to do that again. I swung my bat back and forth, unlocking my wrists.

Kearney sidearmed me again. I stayed with the pitch, but checked my swing as the ball went wide.

"Ball," the ump said.

"Way to look them over, Tim," Mr. Herndon called out. "Make him work out there."

Kearney glanced at Boomer and sidearmed me for the third time in a row. I ducked at the last second and it just missed my head.

"Good reflexes, Tim," Casey Birdwell said to me, grinning, as though we were old friends. "Last year Kearney busted a guy's skull who didn't have good reflexes. And you know what? Now the guy's got no reflexes at all."

I laughed. Casey was a talking catcher.

Kearney went to his stretch, and pitched overhand. It was close and I jumped back.

"He's wild today," Casey said sadly.

"Three and one," the ump said.

I looked at my Dad. He clapped his hands. No signs. I was on my own. I dug in. It would have to be in there before I'd swing. We needed base runners. On the other hand, Steve Glazko was up next. Then Scopus. Neither of them were good hitters.

Kearney went to a full wind-up on the next pitch and Boomer took advantage of it, jumping off for second. He had the big jump. I didn't swing. The ball was in for a strike. Casey didn't throw down and Boomer was on second. One out. Our bench talked it up.

I dug in. Kearney was fussed. He kicked the dirt and looked back at second now and again. He took his time. When I was out there pitching and things were going badly, I hurried things up. Not so Kearney. He did a thousand little things to get himself composed again.

Boomer tried to rattle him. He took a big lead. Kearney looked at him and then stepped off the rubber. Boomer got back to second.

"Forget about him, Kearn," Casey called out. "Nine runs ahead. Let's get the wild pitcher out."

Kearney nodded, and again went to the full wind-up. I saw Boomer take off out of the corner of my eye. The pitch came down. I swung. Late. The ball slithered off the end of my bat. A squiggler down the first base line. It was going to be a close one. Kearney was running over. Their first baseman was running in. The second baseman was running for first. I was slow. Too slow. They were going to get me. All of a sudden, someone, their shortstop maybe, yelled: "Home."

Kearney had the ball. He looked from me toward home. I didn't see what happened then. Later I found out that Boomer had pretended he was going to come crashing home. It was the greatest fake in the history of Arborville Recreation Department baseball. Kearney threw home. Boomer whirled and dashed back to third and made it with a headfirst dive ahead of the throw from Casey. I crossed first safely.

Boomer's clever base running had got me a base hit.

The Warren Plumbers' bench was up and shouting.

My jubilance dropped fast, though. Steve Glazko, a little guy with glasses, was up now and I'd yet to see him hit a ball out of the infield.

"Look alive, Foster," Mr. Herndon called out.

I looked at him. He nodded toward third. Wake up, Tim, I thought. My father was sending me signals.

He hitched up his belt in the middle of a flurry of gestures. Steal. With nine runs behind? Maybe he wanted to rattle Kearney. I saw their third baseman looking at my father. Dad took off his cap. All signs wiped off.

Kearney pitched from a stretch. Outside. A pitchout. Casey expected me to go down, but I stood there. He hesitated and then called time and trotted out to the mound. Dad watched them. When Casey got back, he gave me a flurry of signals including a belt hitch and at the end again took off his cap wiping them all out.

I knew he was figuring they were certain I'd go down and that the moment the catcher threw to second, Boomer would take off for home.

Kearney threw to the plate. Wide again. Casey jumped up and whipped the ball toward second. The shortstop took the throw halfway in, behind the pitcher, and he threw it right back at Casey who grabbed it and stood there waiting—for nothing. Boomer was standing on third, chewing his bubble gum, and I was still on first. And little Steve Glazko had two balls and no strikes going for him.

It was the turn of our bench to laugh. Kearney turned red. He and Casey had another conference. It was hard to believe they had a nine-run lead. I heard Casey tell him to calm down and just throw it in there.

As soon as Casey got back, Dad gave me the steal signal, rubbing his hands together, and there was no wipe-off. He knew Kearney was upset and there wouldn't be any more pitchouts. Kearney threw. I took off for second. The ball was in the dirt. Casey blocked it and I took second standing up.

Kearney was furious. Our bench was riding him now. His fourth pitch was a ball and Steve was on. Bases loaded and only one out. Tom Scopus, another poor hitter, was up.

He looked down to third. Dad touched elbows, hands on hips, touched his knees—the bunt signal.

Kearney went to his full wind-up, and Scopus bunted. It was the last thing they were expecting from a team nine runs behind.

Boomer was halfway home when Tom's bat made contact with the ball. I was on my way to third. The ball dribbled out to the mound. Kearney leaped for it. There was no play at home. He looked at third, and by the time he looked to first there was only a second left. He threw it as hard as he could. It went four feet over the first baseman's head. I came home on the overthrow. Steve took third and Scopus was on second with a single followed by a throwing error.

The score was nine to two, but you'd have thought we'd beaten them by the way our bench was cheering.

Mario's bench was silent. Finally one of them said: "What're you guys yelling about? You're seven runs behind and all you got is one hit this inning."

"We got two runs on that hit and we're gonna get more," Art Tippit shouted.

Bill Wilson, our right fielder, was ninth in the batting order. A thin boy with freckles, he batted left-handed. You could tell he wasn't really a ball player. He played behind Paul Nisbet when Paul was playing his regular right field position.

"He's a looker, Kearney," Casey sang out. "Seven-run lead, big Kearn. Blow it by him."

Kearney threw his fast ball and Bill, swinging late, sliced it. It looped lazily over the third baseman's head, and fell into left field. A cheap hit. Steve scored and Tom Scopus in his excitement slid into third even though there was no play on him. Bill Wilson stood on first beaming from ear to ear. "Did you see that?" he asked anyone who would listen, "I hit that ball. I never got a hit before in a game."

"You never will again," the first baseman growled.

Nine to three and still only one man out. There were runners on first and third and the top of the batting order was coming up.

Mario's coach stood up, undecided as to whether to visit the mound or not. He decided against it and cupped his hands, shouting at Kearney to forget about the runners and just chuck hard. They were cheap lucky hits.

"We're a cheap lucky team," Tom Scopus said happily.

Art Tippit came up. He swung a choked bat. Kearney checked the runner on third and threw to the plate. Bill Wilson, who'd never stolen a base in his life, took off for second like a jackrabbit. Casey faked a throw to second and fired the ball to third. Scopus dove back into the bag safely.

"Boy, we got them worried," Randy Green said. "Be a hero, Art. Two big ones on base."

"Bring those chickens home, Art," Boomer called out.

I looked over to where Tad, Ralph, Willie, and Howard were sitting. They were silent, watching as though they couldn't believe what was happening.

Kearney went to the full wind-up. Scopus took a lead on the stretch but didn't move off the bag, though I could hear my father telling him to. That throw from Casey had scared old Tom.

The pitch was on its way. Art popped it up and Kearney grabbed it and now there were two out. Paul Nisbet was at bat.

"Keep it going, Paul."

"Bring those guys in, Nisbet."

"Be tough up there, Paul."

Paul was first pitch swinging and he hit it solidly. A line shot over third. We started to cheer but their shortstop dove to his right and backhanded it, a beautiful catch. I could see why they raved about Marchessini. Our big inning was over and our rally had fallen six runs short.

Mr. Herndon clapped us on the backs. "Good inning, boys. Hold them now, and we'll get those runs back."

"We never got even one run off Kearney before," Randy Green said, trotting out past me.

The ump handed me the ball. Paul Nisbet was putting on his equipment. There was no one out there to warm me up. I saw Dad grab a catcher's glove, and then Tad Myers come running down from the tall grass.

"Can I warm Tim up, Mr. Foster?" he asked.

"Sure," Dad said, with a smile.

So Tad warmed me up. He squatted down and made a target and I threw to it. He pegged it back at me hard.

"Nice throwing, Tim," he said quietly. "You're going to beat these guys."

"I hope so. You got on another team yet?"

"No."

"We could sure use you guys."

Tad didn't say anything. He whipped the ball back at me and then Paul came up. Tad handed him the glove.

They looked at each other for a moment.

Tad shrugged. "He looks good."

"We could use another pitcher," Paul said.

Tad nodded but could find no words. He went back to his buddies on Mario's side of the diamond.

Ralph, Howard, Willie, Charley, Kevin, Tad—they didn't look like a happy or gloating bunch any more. They looked like a left-out bunch.

The bottom half of the second was completely different from the first. My nervousness was gone. My arm felt loose; I had made the mound my own. I wasn't pitching out of Kearney's spots. Behind me, the Plumbers were talking things up.

Mario's had quieted down. They weren't jeering at us

any more. I got them out one, two, three. The first guy popped up. I struck out the second, and the third guy hit a line drive right at Boomer.

But if I'd settled down, so had Kearney Boylan. He got us out one, two, three in the next inning.

I had the top of the batting order to contend with. I threw more off speed pitches but mixed them better with the fast balls and I tried to give both pitches the same motion. Marchessini got a single, but I struck out the next two batters and Steve Glazko caught a pop-up. They were swinging under my fast ball.

Dad swatted me on the seat as we crossed paths. "You're looking like a pitcher."

"Paul's making me mix them up."

"Keep them humming."

"All right, guys," Mr. Herndon said, clapping his hands, "this is the inning we get our runs back."

I was first up. The third baseman was playing back. I wasn't very fast and they knew it now. Still, there was just a chance.

I bunted it down the third base line. Too hard. I put my head down and ran, but I was thrown out by two steps.

"Good idea, Tim," Mr. Herndon said.

Steve Glazko was up next. To everyone's surprise, he bunted on the very next pitch. The third baseman, surprised, let it roll. It stayed fair and Steve was on.

We began talking it up.

Kearney bore down and struck out Tom Scopus. And this time he pitched inside to left-handed batter Bill Wilson, not giving him another chance to slice to the opposite field. Bill popped it up off the handle. Kearney kept a mental book on batters. He knew which guys had gotten hits off him before, the kind of pitches they'd hit and where they'd hit them. I'd have to learn to do this if I was to be a pitcher.

My arm still felt loose and I got the Supermarket team one, two, three. My fast ball was rising slightly and they were under it.

We came into the fourth inning, still six runs behind, with the top of our batting order up.

Art Tippit worked Kearney to three and two before he grounded out, with the pitcher throwing to first. Then Paul was up. Kearney tried to blow it by him but Paul had a nice, smooth, short swing; he timed the pitch beautifully and hit it over second base for a single.

"Here we go, gang," Randy said. "C'mon, Bobby, bring him home."

It seemed to me Kearney was slowing down a little. This was the first practice game of the season, and he was probably only supposed to go four innings.

The Mario's coach came out to talk with Kearney, and my dad took advantage of the time out to talk with Bobby Herndon. He waved Paul to come in and the three of them had a meeting. I wondered what was going on and asked Mr. Herndon. He smiled and said:

"I don't know what your dad's cooking up, Tim, but he knows baseball and it's good enough for me."

What Dad was cooking up became evident on the next pitch. Hit and run. Paul took off for second and Bobby hit behind him. The ball shot through the gap between first and second. Paul went all the way round to third.

Mr. Herndon smiled. "Hit and run, six runs behind. Well,

it worked and it woke us up so let's keep it going. Bring them home, Boomer."

Their outfielders backed up for Boomer. He was one of the best hitters in the league.

On the first pitch to the plate, Bobby took off for second. With a fast runner on third, Casey didn't even throw it down to second. He just held onto it.

"OK, Kearn," he called out. "Let's get the Boomer. We've got six runs on them."

Kearney breathed out with a sigh. "He's getting tired," Mr. Herndon said. "We ought to get some runs off him before they bring in Marchessini."

"Marco's got a curve ball," Bill Wilson said to me. "A real curve."

Boomer took a pitch inside, then a strike inside. The third pitch was right down the middle and Boomer really laid into it. It shot between the center fielder and the left fielder and it had home run labeled all over it. Boomer came home standing up. In fact, the ball almost rolled into the nature pond near the high school parking lot.

We pounded Boomer after he crossed the plate. A three-run homer. The score was now nine to six. Only three runs behind.

"Time, Ump," Mario's coach said. He went out and that was all for Kearney Boylan. An awed silence spread over our bench. It was the first time Kearney Boylan had ever been knocked out of a baseball game. The big guy came out and moved over to play first base. The first baseman moved to short, and Tom Marchessini came in to pitch.

He wasn't nearly as fast as Boylan, but he had control and everyone kept saying he had a wicked curve.

My father and the next batter Randy Green were having a quick meeting and I guessed Dad was telling Randy to take one: always take one on a new pitcher, let him search for the strike zone, and look at his stuff.

Marchessini didn't have to struggle much for the strike zone. He got two quick strikes on Randy.

"C'mon, Randy," Mr. Herndon called out, "let's swing that bat."

Randy had taken called third strikes both his other times at bat. This time he did it too.

My turn now. As I came to the plate, the voices came across the field from Mario's side, but to my astonishment the message was different.

"You can hit him, Tim."

"Hit one out of here, big Tim."

"Go get'm, Tim."

Behind Mario's bench, our bunch of ex-Plumbers were talking it up for us! Tad Myers, Howard Kohn, Charley Burns . . . and then there was Ralph Weyland calling out to me:

"Give it a ride, Tim boy."

I couldn't believe my ears. Even Willie Warner was shouting encouraging things.

The guys on the Mario's bench turned around, annoyed. "Hey," one said, "didn't they kick you off that team?"

"We quit," Ralph said.

"Then quit rooting for them."

"We can root for whomever we want."

"If you're going to make noises for them," Mario's coach said, "then move over to their side of the field."

Mr. Herndon laughed. "Mario's are coming apart. Now's

the time to hop on them. A little bingle, Tim. Keep it go-ing."

I didn't step right in. Like everyone else, I was fascinated, as six boys got up from the grass, mounted their bicycles, and came around to our side of the field, shouting encouragement at me as they rode.

"All right," the Ump said, "let's get a batter in there."

I felt goose-pimply all over, and happy as I stepped into the batter's box. Now dig in, I told myself and get a hit!

Marchessini's first pitch was right at my head. I stepped back. The ball curved.

"Strike one," the Ump said.

"You're not down in Illinois, buddy," Casey sang out, "we throw curves up here."

The next pitch was right at me again, instinctively I ducked back. Again it curved. The ump called: "Strike two."

"Be tough in there, Tim," my father called out.

I'd never hit against a curve ball before. It was hard to believe anyone our age could throw a curve, but there it was.

I was determined to hang in there on the next one. Marchessini went to his wind-up. I waited for the ball at my head. To my surprise, it came in low and outside and fast. I watched it go by.

"Strike three," the ump said.

"It was outside," I was going to say to the ump, but stopped myself. Maybe it was and maybe it wasn't, but the big thing was he'd fooled me and I knew it. Complaining to the ump wasn't going to make me look any better.

No one said anything to me as I walked back to the bench.

They were talking it up for Steve Glazko, the next batter. Steve took a ball and a strike and then he topped the ball down the third base line and was thrown out by ten feet. We were still three runs behind and had only two innings in which to catch up.

"Well, well, well," Art Tippit said, as he went to get his glove, "look what's joined us."

Sitting behind us, on a grassy knoll were the ex-Plumbers. Ralph Weyland blushed.

"Do you guys mind if we watch from here?"

"It's a free country," Tom Scopus said.

"Hold'm, guys," Tad Meyers said. "You can get those runs back."

"Good hit, Boomer," Howard Kohn said. "You almost hit it into the pond."

Ralph blocked my way as I started out to the mound. "You're pitching a good game, Foster." He held out his hand.

I took it.

"Thanks."

"Hey, what is this? A tea party? We're three runs behind. Let's hustle out there."

Mr. Herndon growled the words, but I could tell he was pleased the six had come over to our side of the field.

Could it be a lucky omen? We'd find out soon enough.

»13«

A Battle's Not a War

During my third warm-up pitch of that inning I felt it—a little twinge in my shoulder. Just a kink, I thought. I didn't feel it again on the other two warm-up pitches.

Mario's first man up was their right fielder. I tried to remember what he'd done before. I'd got him out twice, but on what kinds of pitches? High or low? Fast or slow?

Paul signaled for a fast ball and moved his glove slightly outside. He remembered. I threw my pitch and let go of it too late. It was way wide.

"He'll walk you, Johnny."

Paul waggled one finger again and held his target over the middle. I threw it hard down the middle and as the ball left my fingertips I felt that twinge again in my shoulder.

The batter swung and the ball came right back at me like

a shot. I put up my glove to defend myself and the ball stuck in the webbing. For a second I didn't know I had it. Then I tossed it to Bobby who tossed it around the infield.

Paul came trotting out. "You OK?"

"Sure. Why?"

"That last ball didn't have much zip on it."

"I'll get some on the rest."

He went back and squatted down. Paul waggled one finger on the next batter. I threw it as hard as I could and winced. The batter laid a bunt down the third base line. Quick as a cat Paul pounced on it and whipped it over to first. Two away.

My arm felt as though it was ready to come off. Paul knew something was wrong, but no one else did. The others thought things were good. Mr. Herndon was marking his score card, but my father was watching me closely.

Paul waggled one finger. I shook my head. He waggled two.

I threw it up there soft and the guy really stepped into it. Lucky for us he hit it high too, and toward center field. Boomer, great wonderful bubble-gum-chewing Boomer, got a jump on the ball and he caught it over his shoulder. The side was out.

Everyone patted me as I came in.

Dad stopped me. "How's the arm?"

"OK," I said.

"Are you sure?"

"Positive."

"You looked like you were pushing a little on those last pitches. No one expects you to go all the way, Tim. Don't stay in long enough to hurt your arm."

"I'm feeling fine, Dad."

I wanted to go all the way, to show the guys I could pitch a complete game. I wasn't doing too well with the bat, I couldn't run, and I had let them hit me all over the place in the first inning. We were on our way back now and Bobby wasn't a pitcher. I had to finish this game. For me and for the team.

It was the top of the sixth. We had this inning and the next to get those runs back. Scopus, Wilson, and Tippit were up—the eighth, ninth, and lead off batter.

Marchessini was throwing tantalizing low curve balls. Tom waved his bat three times and sat down. Bill Wilson, who was proving to have more of a hitting eye than anyone expected, was next up. He was our only left-handed batter now that Willie Warner was off the team. I figured Bill had a better chance against this pitcher with the right-handed curve than we did. Marchessini's curves would be bending into Bill.

Marchessini must have thought so too because he threw two quick fast balls over the outside corner for strikes.

Then he threw one in the dirt—a curve ball. Bill hit the next pitch into the hole between third and short. The shortstop knocked it down, but he had no play at first.

It woke up our team. Everyone was noisy again. Art Tippit was up. Dad gave him the bunt signal. It would be a two-out bunt, but the idea was to get two men into scoring position. Marchessini was easier to bunt against than Kearney because he threw low pitches.

Art bunted down the first base line. Bill took off for second and drew the second baseman with him. Kearney Boylan came in from first to field the ball, whirled, but he had no one to throw it to—it was a fielding lapse by the second baseman who should have covered first on the bunt. All the Plumbers were safe, and the Mario's team was hollering at their second baseman.

"Now's the time to take them," Mr. Herndon called out. "Paul, this pitcher is your meat. Wait on the curve. He'll hang it up for you nice and fat."

Marchessini was unruffled, though. He got Paul to beat two curve balls into the dirt and then he threw a high fast ball. Paul went fishing, and our opportunity was over.

"Think you can hold them, Tim?" Mr. Herndon asked me.

"Yes, sir."

"Your dad thought your arm might be tightening up."

"I'm OK."

"No pain when you throw?"

"No, sir," I lied. This was a different kind of lie than the others. This was for the sake of the team.

"OK, Son. Go get them."

Tad Myers was behind the plate, ready to warm me up while Paul put on his equipment.

"Fire away, Tim," he said, grinning at me.

I gave Tad a fast one and the pain shot through my whole arm.

"What's the matter?" he asked. My face had registered what my arm had felt.

"Nothing," I said, but I let up on my other pitches and when Tad gave the glove back to Paul I heard him say Tim was getting tired and Paul said there was no one else to pitch.

As yet Mario's didn't know my arm was going. They only

knew that after that disastrous first inning, I'd held them pretty well. They weren't as cocky as they'd been at the start of the game. If I could continue to hold them, we would get those runs back. The heart of our batting order was up next inning. Bobby . . . Boomer . . .

Marchessini stepped into the batter's box, reminding me that the heart of *their* batting order was up now.

To my dismay, Paul signaled for a fast ball. I wouldn't be able to throw it. My arm felt as though it was practically detached, held on only by a string, like a broken doll's arm.

I went to a full wind-up, kicked and threw it. At the last second I took something off it to save my arm. The wind-up must have fooled Marchessini because he was out in front of it, and fouled it off.

"Good pitch, Tim," Mr. Herndon called out.

I kicked some dirt around. A guy could only get away with a pitch like that once. Then he had to really throw it fast to keep the batter honest.

Paul waggled the one finger again. How I hated that one finger. Always the fast balls that hurt you, that tear your shoulder off. Even though I wasn't hot, I was sweating. The game had already gone on too long, during this cool spring day and everyone was silent, watching. I felt lonelier pitching on that mound than I'd ever felt being on the outside of a game.

I went to the full wind-up and again I took something off it. Again Marchessini was in front of it and fouled it off.

But how many times could a pitcher get away with this?

"Time, ump," Paul said, and trotted out.

"Are you OK, Tim?"

"No."

"What's the matter?"

"My arm hurts."

"We'd better call Mr. Herndon out here."

"What for? There's no one else to pitch."

Paul nodded. "Ever throw sidearm?"

"No."

"Try it. Sometimes that's easier on the arm than the three quarters overhand. Try sidearming Marchessini on this one."

Paul trotted back. On our bench, Mr. Herndon and my father were conferring. Behind them, the ex-Plumbers were sitting silently. Tad Meyers was looking at me anxiously. If only he were in uniform, on the team—he could come in and finish up the game.

Paul squatted down and waggled the one finger. Sidearm and good luck, I thought.

I wound up and tried my first sidearm pitch. It didn't hurt as much but the ball flew wide of the plate and back to the backstop.

"He's finished up there, Marco," someone shouted. "His arm's shot."

Paul retrieved the ball.

"Time, ump," Mr. Herndon said and came out to the mound.

"Does your arm hurt, Tim?"

"A little."

"When did it start?"

"Last inning."

"You should have told the truth when your dad asked you. I could have warmed up Bobby. Now he'll have to go in cold."

"I can throw half-speed OK, Mr. Herndon."

"You can hurt your arm just throwing, Tim. Bobby, come over here."

"Please don't take me out, Mr. Herndon."

"Tim, you can't pitch with a sore arm. You pitch now and you won't be able to pitch again for a month, maybe not the whole summer. Ump, I'm changing pitchers. Bobby, warm up. Tim, go out to right field. Randy, come in and play third."

"What about Tad?" I asked. "Couldn't he pitch?"

"If he were on the team he could. Loosen up, Bob. How many pitches can he have, ump?"

"I'll give him twelve pitches, Doug," the ump said. "Otherwise we could be here all day."

"Fair enough. Tim, you pitched a fine game. I hope next time you'll let me know truthfully how your arm feels when it hurts."

He was annoyed with me, and rightfully so. I hadn't thought about Bobby being able to warm up between innings. It all proved that fibs didn't pay off even when you thought you were doing it for the sake of others.

I went out to right field. Mario's bench started their usual round of catcalls.

"Hey, Herndon, you look great for a third baseman."

"Let's see your meat ball, Bobby."

"He even pitches like a plumber."

While Bobby was warming up, Boomer and I threw a ball back and forth. That is, Boomer threw flies to me while I rolled the ball back on the ground to him.

"Hey, guys, look at the new right fielder. He can't throw. Hit it out to right, Marco."

"Batter up," the ump said.

"What's the count, ump?"

"One ball and two strikes."

"Hit it out of there, Marco."

"No batter, Bobby boy. No batter."

I knew that in the major leagues it was not unusual for a third baseman to become a pitcher. You needed a strong arm to play third. Bobby's was strong but it wasn't a pitcher's arm.

His first pitch was high. Two and two. His next pitch was wide. Three and two. And his third pitch sailed over Paul's head. Marchessini was on, Kearney Boylan was up.

Bobby didn't know how to keep a man on. He went to a full wind-up and Marchessini stole second easily. Bobby's pitch was in the dirt and Paul did a good job blocking it.

Again Bobby went to a full wind-up and Marchessini took off for third. Kearney Boylan swung on the pitch and hit it over Bill Wilson's head in left field for a home run. The score was now eleven to six.

That was only the beginning. Casey hit Bobby's first pitch between me and Boomer. Boomer cut it off, whirled and threw to Art Tippit at second. They had Casey dead, but Art took his eyes off the throw, probably listening to Casey's big feet coming down the baseline. The ball went by him and Casey was on second.

There's no use in telling it in any more detail. Before that inning was over, Mario's got three more runs on walks and hits, and the score was 14-6. We were back to where we were in the first inning.

When we came up for our last licks we were eight runs behind, with Marchessini looking like he could throw those low curve balls all day.

Bobby, Boomer, and Randy were up.

"Let's go, Plumbers. We can get those runs back."

"Be a hitter up there, Bobby."

Bobby was a hitter. He singled between short and third, and then Boomer hit a fly ball that dropped behind Kearney at first. We had men on first and second.

Randy had been a strike-out victim all day long. He was due. Everyone was on him not to look at any more strikes, and so he swung at the first pitch, a bad pitch and dribbled it down the line toward third. The third baseman had to come in to make the play. Hoping for a force out at third, he had been playing back. When he came in and picked up the ball he made the mistake of looking back at third, as though the shortstop would be covering for him. The shortstop wasn't. Now he had only one play left, at first. And Randy was fast. He threw hurriedly and high. The ball pulled Kearney off the bag. Bases were loaded, with nobody out. Our bench exploded. Everyone was yelling.

"C'mon, Tim. Give it a ride."

"Win your game, Tim."

"Show them that pitchers can hit, Tim."

"He's not pitching now, he's playing the outfield."

"Show him outfielders can hit, Tim."

"Who said they couldn't?"

"Shut up and pull for Foster."

My father cupped his hands. "Stay with the curve, Tim," he called out.

I hadn't really hit the ball all day. Determination rose in me to stay with Marchessini's curve and be alert for that quick little fast ball of his.

He curved me on the first pitch. The ball came right at

me and I hung in there. It started to break. I went with it and my bat came around. Solid wood. On the ground. Please, God, let it go through. I heard everyone yelling at me.

"Run, Tim, run."

I ran as hard as I could without knowing where the ball was. And then suddenly it appeared in front of me. It was over my head, in Kearney Boylan's glove. I had hit into a double play. Marchessini had gone into the hole between third and short, speared my hot grounder, whipped it home and Casey had whipped it to first. A double play.

I felt like crying. I had hit the ball solidly.

"Tough chance, Tim," said Art Tippit who was coaching at first.

I didn't say anything, just went off to the side and sat down in the grass. Our side of the field was quiet. Steve Glazko was up next. He fouled off one pitch and then popped up to Marchessini to end the game. It was all over. I'd failed on the mound and at the plate.

"Hey, fella," a voice said. "Wake up." I looked up. It was Kearney Boylan towering over me. He'd come over from first base. "Here, have a hand up."

He extended a big hand. When I was up he patted my right arm gently.

"You'll be all right, Foster."

Marchessini appeared in front of me. He held out his hand. "Tough game, Tim," he said. "It'll be different when your arm's better."

"Thanks. You played a good game."

And then there was Casey, grinning and swatting me on the shoulders as if he and I were old friends. "Now don't you go learn any curve balls, Timmy. You're tough enough as it is."

The rest of their team were there too, shaking hands, saying "good game." Even their coach said, "You'll win a lot of games before this season is over, Son." Turning to my father he added, "Your boy's got an arm on him."

Dad smiled. "We'll have to put some liniment on it."

"Boys," Mr. Herndon said, "hustle in."

It was odd, crazy, losing by eight runs, to have everyone saying "good game" as if it had been close and shaking my hand as though I'd done well.

"All right, Plumbers," Mr. Herndon said, when we were all on the bench. "There's no need to be feeling sorry about this game. We gave them the fight of their lives and they know it."

"Gee, Mr. Herndon, we lost by eight runs," Bill Wilson said.

"Take away two innings," Mr. Herndon said, "and it was an even game. I think we lost the battle today, but we might win the war. We'll win because we've found ourselves a pitcher. I want to set up practice for Tuesday. I—"

He paused and looked over our heads.

"What're you boys hanging around for?"

He was speaking to the ex-Plumbers.

Tad Myers cleared his throat. "We feel we've made a mistake, Mr. Herndon. We want to know if we can join the team again."

Mr. Herndon's face was impassive. "All of you?" he asked.

"Yes."

"You too, Ralph?"

Ralph Weyland turned red, but he nodded.

"What made you change your mind?"

"We found we were rooting for our team," Howard said.

"Is that all?"

"No," Tad said quietly. "We found we were all wrong about Tim. He's got more guts than all of us put together. We want to be on any team he's on."

"I made a mistake, Mr. Herndon," Ralph said. "I want to apologize for it."

"No apologies," Mr. Herndon said gruffly. "Fortunately for you, I haven't met with the league president yet. However, I think I ought to let the question of your rejoining the team be answered by your teammates. Some of them may lose some playing time when you come back. How do you boys feel about this?"

"I'll take them back," Bill Wilson chirped. "I got two hits off Kearney Boylan. I'm not so sure Willie's going to get his position back."

"I'm not so sure either. Art?"

"I'll vote them back, Mr. Herndon," Tippit said.

"Paul?"

"Man," Paul said with a grin and a nod toward Charley Burns, "that catching is hard work."

"Bobby?"

Bobby shrugged. "OK," he said.

"Randy?"

Randy hesitated before answering. He hadn't done well today. He was pretty sure he'd never start when the ex-Plumbers came back on the team.

"Oh, it's OK with me if it's OK with the other guys."

"Steve?"

"Sure."

"Tom?"

Scopus scratched his head and grinned. "Let's fine them first."

Everyone laughed.

"And then?" Mr. Herndon asked.

Tom thought it over. "Well, with Tad *and* Tim pitching we could go all the way."

Mr. Herndon looked at me. "Tim, since you started the whole thing, how do you feel about it?"

They all looked at me. Just yesterday the ex-Plumbers were looking at me waiting for me to decide whether to quit or not. Now they were waiting for me to decide about their coming back on the team.

"What about it, Tim?" Mr. Herndon said.

"I'd like to see the Plumbers all together again."

"So be it," Mr. Herndon said. "What's past is past. We're all together again, but with some changes. Bill Wilson looked pretty good at the plate today. Willie, you'll have to beat him out for that job. The same goes for Kevin and Steve Glazko, for Howard Kohn and Art Tippit at second. Ralph, this is true for you and Tom Scopus as well. The boys who played today are starting until you others prove it otherwise. Practice Tuesday, 4 P.M. We'll go over some of the mistakes we made today. Wait—before you break up, I want to say this . . ."

He paused.

"I was proud of you boys today. You stood up to the best team in the league and scared them pretty good. You knocked the best pitcher in the league out of the box. Even though you fell apart, you came together again. Today you became a ball club. We'll win some, lose some, but today you came of age and I was proud of you. Tim, no more throwing for all of next week. Get your dad to rub some liniment in your arm. Bobby, you and Randy get the equipment together. Everybody lend a hand. Mr. Foster and I can give those without bikes rides home."

Tad and the others were getting on their bicycles. We looked at them and they looked at us.

It shouldn't break up like this, I thought. We ought to go home together.

"I'd just as soon walk home," I said.

"Me too," Tom Scopus said.

"Let's all walk," Steve Glazko said.

Mr. Herndon looked at us and then at my father. "I guess they didn't work hard enough," he said solemnly.

My father smiled. "I'll give you a hand with the equipment," he said.

»14«

A Team United

So we were all together again. Fifteen of us, six on bicycles, nine walking. Six in street clothes, nine in baseball uniforms . . . but all of us a team.

Everyone felt so good about it that no one said anything. We walked down Stadium Boulevard, past the golf course. We cut across the Baer Machine parking lot and over the railroad tracks toward Granger Avenue where we would begin to split up and go home.

Like branches of a tree, we would break up slowly. But now, as we walked toward Granger, everyone felt the unity.

Paul said: "I don't think Kearney will ever beat us again."

"He didn't look so big today," Steve said.

Tad smiled. "It's we who've got bigger. I was thinking that as we were watching. We looked as big as they did."

"Great home run, Boomer."

"I didn't get a hit when we needed it. I've got to practice hitting curves."

"My dad'll throw us curves in practice," I said.

"Your old man's the best third base coach we ever had," Art Tippit said. "He outguessed them each time."

"Wilson, how come you hit the ball like you did today?"

Bill grinned happily. "You know what Casey said to me? He said if I ever got a hit off Kearney again he'd bust me in the mouth."

We all laughed and then I had to listen to some advice on how to cure my aching arm.

"Don't do anything tonight, Tim. Don't even lift a fork. Use your left hand."

"Take a hot shower."

"No, a cold shower."

"I've got some liniment I can lend you."

"Sleep on your left side."

I laughed. "With all this advice, I'd better feel fine in a hurry."

"So long, guys," Scopus said. "See you in school Monday."

"Hey, don't forget to bring your soccer ball, Tom."

"I won't. Good game."

"Good game, Tom."

Tom left, and then Steve and Bobby Herndon left us, and then Randy, Willie, and Paul Nisbet.

Bill Wilson said good-bye, and Boomer Gohane and Howard Kohn went off together. Howard shook hands with me.

"I hope your arm feels better, Tim."

"It'll be OK."

Howard turned to Art Tippit who had played his second base position. "I hope your arm feels worse."

Art laughed. "It's feeling better every day."

"So long, guys. Good game."

"Good game, Boomer. Good game."

Then it was Art Tippit's turn to leave, and Charley and Kevin and Ralph. Ralph turned to me. "Foster . . ." he began. But he didn't know how to finish it. Besides it had all been said at the diamond. The past was past.

"See you in school Monday," I said to Ralph.

"I'll see you first in the soccer game," he said with a grin. "Good game, you guys."

"Thanks. So long."

And then it was just me and Tad Myers walking alone. Tad rode his bicycle slowly; I walked alongside.

"What made you guys come to the game today?" I asked.

"Ralph wanted to see the slaughter."

"What made you start rooting for us?"

"When you guys didn't quit. When you fought back the way you did. We found ourselves cheering for you before we knew it."

"It made us feel good."

"I'm glad, because we were wrong."

"So was I. About your glove."

"It's over now. Hey, you want to come over after supper and play a little Ping-Pong?"

"I'll ask my dad."

"Your dad's nice, Tim."

"I know," I said. "I'm a lucky guy."

"See you later, I hope. And—Good game, Tim."

"Thanks, Tad."

He biked off, and then it was just me . . . alone but not lonely. I was now a part of a team, a part of a new town.

I cut across the park—still my favorite shortcut. There weren't many people about, just a few tennis players at the far end, and some little kids on swings, and the usual dogs chasing each other in circles.

I felt like I'd lived here all my life.